Gunslinger

by

Cynthia Breeding

This is a work of fiction. Names, characters, places, and incidents are either the product of the author's imagination or are used fictitiously, and any resemblance to actual persons living or dead, business establishments, events, or locales, is entirely coincidental.

Gunslinger

COPYRIGHT © 2024 by Cynthia Breeding

Cover Art by *Teddi Black*

The Wild Rose Press, Inc.
PO Box 708
Adams Basin, NY 14410-0708
Visit us at www.thewildrosepress.com

Publishing History
First Edition, 2025
Trade Paperback ISBN 978-1-5092-6088-1
Digital ISBN 978-1-5092-6089-8

Published in the United States of America

Chapter One

San Francisco, 1879

Abigail Clayton stepped onto the Long Wharf platform and brushed flecks of cinder off the shoulder of her pelisse. She tried not to choke on the sooty smoke spewing from the locomotive's stack.

Criminy. The train journey from New York had been an exhausting eight days even though the conductors bragged about the speed of the latest engine. Her bones had been rattled by the clanking of iron wheels on metal tracks, her teeth practically jarred loose, and every muscle ached. All Abby wanted was a hot bath and a real bed instead of a hard bench for a berth.

But first, she needed to find her husband...if only she knew what he looked like.

Opening her reticule, she took out two pieces of paper and carefully unfolded them. The one was her marriage-by-proxy, which had been quickly signed by a magistrate in the Bowery with two strangers for witnesses. The other was the reply she'd received when she answered an ad for a mail-order bride to come West.

My dearest Miss Clayton,

I hope I may call you 'my dearest' since I pray that you will do me the honor of becoming my wife. Although I am quite the successful entrepreneur—I own a general store that profits nicely from both miners and the local population—I find that I am quite lonely. Virtuous, demure, and refined young ladies are in short supply here. I am sure we will suit quite nicely. I look forward to greeting you at the train station.

Your future grateful companion forever,
Travis Sayer

Abby repressed a very unladylike snort. She was none of those things. She may have hedged a bit in her response to the ad. Oh, her physical *virtue* was intact, but growing up in a tenement with no father, and a mother who took in laundry before she died two years ago, didn't lend itself to being refined. Or demure, although she supposed she could thank her natural inquisitiveness for catching the attention of the Sisters of Mercy who ministered to the poor. They'd seen to it that she and her brother, Ben, had an education.

For all the good it did. Ben was currently serving a sentence for robbery. She'd almost been caught too, which was part of the reason she was here.

This was going to be a new life. A new beginning.

Abby collected her valise—the porter had set it down near her feet—and looked around. One man standing a short distance away caught her attention. He was tall and dressed completely in black, his frockcoat molded to his broad shoulders like a second skin, with a wicked-looking revolver strapped to a muscular thigh. His hair was as black as his clothes and a subtle shadow darkened his jaw, but it was his eyes that struck her. They were the color of whiskey and as penetrating as a wolf's. For a moment their gazes held. Then he turned and walked away.

Abby released the breath she didn't realize she'd been holding. Of course, that man would not be her husband. When Travis had sent the bank check to pay for her transportation, he'd described himself as medium height with blond hair and blue eyes, the same coloring that she had.

There were no blond men on the platform.

Sighing, she walked to the small ticket station at the end of the wharf. She had long ago learned not to count on a man being reliable—the man who'd sired her had been proof of that—but she had hoped that someone who wanted to marry might be different.

"I was supposed to meet someone. Is there a message for a Miss Abigail Clayton?" she asked the young man at the counter.

He shuffled through some papers and then shook his head. "No message, Miss."

This was not a good start. "Where can I hire a hack then? I need to go to Sayer's General Store."

"The hacks are…" The boy stopped. "Did you say *Sayer's* General Store?"

"Yes. Is it far?"

"Not far." The boy paused again. "Is it Travis Sayer you're expectin' to meet?"

Suddenly, her nape began to tingle like it did when she sensed something was very wrong. "Yes. Why?"

He hesitated once more. "There was a brawl in front of McGiver's saloon a couple of weeks ago…well, it turned into a brawl after Mr. Sayer shot a wh-…a woman."

Abby shook her head, sure she hadn't heard correctly. "My hus-…Mr. Sayer shot a woman?"

"One of them painted ones from the dance hall next door. He claimed he'd paid for her company and she didn't want to…" The boy's face turned red. "…do her part."

Abby didn't have to ask what that meant. She'd nearly been forced into the same occupation herself after Ben got arrested. "So what happened then?"

"I heard he grabbed her by the hair and started pulling her down the street. She fought and he pulled his gun."

This was just getting worse. Her intended—Hellfire. Her *husband*—had obviously not been waiting with bated breath for his wife, but he'd also shot a woman who couldn't defend herself. She took a deep breath. "Did he kill her?"

"No. Just an arm wound."

Just. Abby sighed. "I assume I need to take a hack to the local jail then."

The boy looked down. "That won't do you no good."

"Why not?" Her nape tingled again. "Did the constable not arrest him?"

"There weren't no need. Someone in the crowd shot him." The boy looked up. "Mr. Sayer's dead."

****

By the devil's own horns, he hadn't expected Abigail Clayton to be so beautiful. The information he'd gotten on Sayer's new bride hadn't said much. Luke Cameron narrowed his gaze at the woman who'd just stepped off the train. She wore no bonnet and the sun made her golden hair glow like a halo, brightening her eyes to the deep blue of the Pacific. She had the face of an angel, softly rounded, with a pert nose. Not that Luke had any experience with angels. Gunslingers rarely did. But...he studied her face again. Her mouth was definitely not angelic. The full lips, right now gathered in a pout, begged to be kissed. He pushed the thought away. He was here to see who would come for her now that Sayer was dead.

He hadn't meant to kill Sayer, just shoot the gun out of his hand so he couldn't do any more harm than he already had. But the brawl had started so suddenly and he'd been jostled just as he squeezed the trigger. Damnation. He'd wanted the man alive to collect the money Sayer had swindled from several elderly ladies, including his grandmother.

The blonde picked up her valise and looked around. For a moment their eyes met and Luke felt a strange sensation sizzle through him. Something akin to the primal feeling he got when he picked up the trail of whichever fugitive he'd been tracking. Similar, but not the same.

Abruptly, he turned and left. It would be safer to observe from afar.

She wasn't a fugitive, of course, but he hoped she'd be the bait that would lure Sayer's unnamed accomplice in the deceptive scheme to separate unsuspecting souls from their money. That was why he was here. It would be better if Miss Clayton weren't involved at all and just went quietly home.

His connections at Pinkerton's—who hired his fast gun at times—had not been able to get a name on Sayer's partner. The man stayed in the shadows, apparently taking care of all the details, while the charismatic Travis Sayer charmed little old ladies out of their savings.

Luke walked toward the dock where several doxies already lined the pier, waiting for sailors to disembark. From there, he could appear to mingle while keeping an eye on the newly arrived widow.

"Ya sure dun't look like a sailor-boy." One of the women with kohl-lined eyes winked at him. "No' that I mind."

"Ya look like a right-fine gent," said a woman who had the strangest color of red hair he'd ever seen. "I know how to treat a gent."

Another woman looked at the six-gun strapped to his leg and then gave him a leering grin. "Is your other weapon as big?"

He smiled as he sidestepped her hand reaching for him and fished three silver coins out of his pocket. "No need to work today, ladies, although I appreciate your efforts."

They snatched the money with looks of awe. "He really is a gent," he heard one of them say as they scurried away, probably fearful he'd change his mind.

He gazed after them for a moment. He'd heard of San Francisco's Barbary Coast long before he crossed the California border following Sayer. The three-block stretch of Pacific Street between Montgomery and Stockton had as many brothels as it did saloons, and all of them were usually overflowing with miners carrying a bit of gold dust in leather pouches. But the more savvy prostitutes knew sailors coming ashore after weeks or months at sea had their entire wages in their pockets.

He doubted *any* of them actually enjoyed what they did. He strongly doubted it, which was one reason he preferred widows who liked their independence but missed the pleasures of bed sport. And thinking of widows...

Luke turned his attention back to Abigail Clayton, who was now at the row of hired hacks. Apparently, the accomplice was not about to make himself known. Luke sighed as the driver snapped the reins and the carriage moved away. He was going to have to make the acquaintance of Abigail Clayton after all.

****

As Abby stepped through the doorway of Sayer's General Store, various smells assailed her. To her left, the tanginess of brine in a pickle barrel, the sharpness of a cheese wheel on a board covered with a linen, the sweetness of a molasses jar left open, the aroma of coffee beans, and the earthiness of root vegetables in bushel baskets on the floor. To her right, the mustiness of coiled hemp rope as well as the subtler scent of leather boots and bridles. Walking farther inside, she gazed around. Various axes, hammers, shovels, and tin pans were stacked along the left wall and towards the back stood tables with bolts of cloth and a wooden rack with ready-made clothing.

All in all, a very good inventory. The seed of an idea that had come to her on the carriage ride from the train station began to take roots.

"Help you find something, miss?"

She turned as a middle-aged man came from behind the counter that was just to the right of the door. She hadn't noticed him when she entered, but then there was nothing really remarkable about him. Of medium height, neither fat nor skinny, he had brown hair and a pleasant-looking face.

"Are you the manager?"

"I tend the shop. The name's John." He puffed up a bit. "I'm fixin' to buy the place now that Sayer's dead."

Abby bit back a retort that he would be doing no such thing. At least, not yet. But growing up in the Bowery had taught her not to act rashly. "The property is for sale?"

"It will be. I started tending the store two years ago. Then when old man Bronson died last year—this used to be *Bronson's* General Store—and Mr. Sayer bought it, I stayed on. Turns a right good profit."

That was excellent news. Her idea to keep the place was fast congealing. She looked around again. "I can see that it would. Did Mr. Sayer not have any relatives who might be interested in keeping it?"

"Nope."

"No…wife?"

John shook his head. "He'd sent off for one of them mail-order brides, but after he got shot I wrote her telling her not to come."

A letter she'd not gotten since she had already left. Perhaps it was time to break the news. "I'm afraid that letter arrived too late."

The man looked puzzled. "What do you mean?"

"I'm the mail-order bride."

Surprise flitted across his face. "You don't say! I reckon you made the long trip for nothing. I can recommend a boarding house if you're wantin' to rest for a day or two before going back."

"That is kind of you, but I won't be returning East."

His features shifted subtly. Most people wouldn't have noticed, but she hadn't survived the streets of New York without being observant. He was wary. Perhaps he had cause to be, given what she was about to say. Abby gave him a benign smile.

"I am planning to run the store myself."

His brows rose. "You?"

She nodded. "Women can hold property in their own names these days."

"Yes, but aren't you forgetting something?"

"What would that be?"

"You were only fixin' to marry Sayer. So you can't inherit anything."

"Actually, I can. I insisted we be married by proxy before I would make the trip." She shrugged slightly. "I am—was—his wife."

"You got proof of that?"

"Of course." She wasn't about to take the paper out of her reticule though. "I can produce it tomorrow, if you want to see it."

"I do." He managed a smile. "Strictly business, of course. I don't want to lose this place to someone who may not be who she claims to be. There's lots of frauds in this town."

"I understand." Unfortunately, she *did* understand. She had her own shady past to hide. One of the reasons she'd insisted on the marriage-by-proxy was to protect herself just in case her past caught up with her present too soon.

"Do you? There are any number of scoundrels who are willing to dupe a woman."

As if she didn't know. Abby paused. Ben had always warned her men's egos were frail. She didn't want to make an enemy of John, so perhaps she should appeal to that ego. "Since you have the experience, I would very much appreciate it if you would stay on and help me learn to run this business. That would benefit both of us, I think."

For a moment, something flickered in his eyes and then was gone. Slowly, he nodded. "I reckon I could."

"Thank you. I'm glad to hear it." She turned to go toward the door. "Now I must see to living quarters."

9

"I'd recommend Bartlett's Boarding House just off Sutter Street. Travis stayed there."

"Thank you, I'll do that."

As she left, Abby felt a sense of relief. She hadn't known what to expect when she arrived at the store. John had taken the news that she'd be keeping the store rather stoically, she thought. At least, she hadn't made an enemy of him.

****

John narrowed his eyes as the bitch left, allowing himself a moment of anger before he carefully schooled his features into the mask of passivity he always wore. It had taken years to perfect the persona of someone who would not be noticed. Years in which Travis had fleeced gullible old people out of their money, which he, John, had then laundered through various methods. Two years ago he'd decided San Francisco was a gold mine—John quietly laughed at the irony of his little joke—just waiting for someone like him to rake in the gold without having to pan for it. Everything was wide open— prostitution, gambling, opium dens—where fools could be easily taken, but it was in smuggling the opium in from Victoria to avoid paying taxes that the real money was made.

And he had barrels of opium pods hidden in the basement below the store.

Their location, not far from the docks or Chinatown but away from the high crime area, made it a perfect place to conduct the drug trade. He wasn't about to let some hoity-toity tart from New York City mess up his plans. But it might look suspicious if something happened to her right after she arrived, so for now he'd bide his time.

The Bartletts didn't know their son, the captain of the *Neptune Maiden*, was involved with bringing the opium in, but it was something John could use to blackmail them if he needed more information on the damn bitch.

He hoped Old Man Bronson had enjoyed his last night's sleep. There had been enough powder in his nighttime toddy to kill a horse.

Chapter Two

Unfortunately, when Abby stepped onto the sidewalk in front of the general store, there wasn't a hack to be seen. She reminded herself that San Francisco wasn't New York. That city was two hundred years older and a certain degree of urbanity had taken hold, even in the Bowery. Hacks for hire were readily available. From what she'd seen on the carriage drive to the store, San Francisco seemed a rough-and-tumble place, full of prospectors and hardy people who could probably walk ten miles without getting tired.

She slipped her small reticule into the pocket of her pelisse and moved the valise from one hand to the other. She'd seen a town square on the way over that didn't seem that far away. She could probably get a hack to take her to Bartlett's Boarding House from there.

Maybe she should have told the one that brought her from the train station to wait, she thought as she walked along, but she hadn't known how long she would be. As it turned out, it hadn't taken her more than a few minutes to establish the store was something of a personal gold mine for her. If she worked hard and studied the accounts and learned the business, she could make something of herself.

Hopefully, John knew *something* about the accounts so she wouldn't have to figure everything out herself. The man had seemed suspicious at first and she guessed she couldn't blame him for that. Having a stranger show up from nowhere to claim the store probably made him think he was going to lose his job. Well, she'd put his mind to rest about that tomorrow. She really did need his expertise, and she'd make sure he realized she respected him. Once he knew she wasn't going to kick him out the door, they'd get along just fine.

She smiled as she turned the corner and saw the bustling area just ahead. Jackson Square, the street sign said. From here she could even see the masts of the merchant ships docked at the wharf. California was indeed a land of opportunity. Here she could finally live an honest life. She didn't need to be wealthy. Just not poor and hungry any more.

Entering the square from Washington Street, she was soon immersed in a moving wall of pedestrians. The crowds reminded her of New York, and she moved her valise in front of her to keep from bumping into people. She hadn't gone far when she spied several hacks across the street, waiting by the curb. As she turned to make her way over to them, someone to her right jostled her, while a person in front of her suddenly tripped.

All of her senses went on high alert even as she felt the ever-so-slight tug on her left side. It was a classic pickpocket routine. The accomplice on the right distracted the victim, the person in front stalled the mark, while the hook—the person who actually did the stealing—moved in from the other side. With lightning quickness, Abby's free arm flashed out and she grabbed a street urchin by his grimy collar.

"I'll have my reticule back, if you please."

The boy looked at her with wide eyes and then over her shoulder. She didn't have to follow his glance to know his partners had already disappeared. She held out her hand. "Now. Before I summon a constable."

Reluctantly, he pulled the small bag out from under his oversized shirt and gave it back. "I'm good, ye know." The boy frowned at her. "How did ye know I done it?"

"Never mind that," she answered. "I'm sure your friends are waiting not far away. Just go."

He didn't need to be told twice. Abby watched as he zigzagged between the pedestrians, bent on getting out of her sight at quickly as possible. She probably should have turned him in, but she didn't have the heart.

In order to put food on the table and to avoid being thrown out of the tenement, Abby and her brother had worked the same scheme too many times to count.

****

Luke's jaw nearly dropped open when he witnessed Miss Abigail Clayton thwart the ragamuffin pickpocket. Such street thievery was practically a profession along the Barbary Coast and he'd have warned her about it had he gotten a chance to meet her. Apparently, she didn't need the advice. He'd never seen anyone—other than a gunslinger drawing his gun—move so quickly. That she'd even detected the attempt also spoke volumes. Where had she grown up that she had developed that kind of sixth sense?

The information on the report he'd been able to obtain, once he'd found Sayer and heard about his plans for a mail-order bride, had been scant. He knew she was from New York City and he'd known when she left. Background information had been sketchy. He'd assumed Sayer wanted a respectable wife for cover, just like the general store served the purpose of making him seem like a respectable businessman. Luke doubted that the bastard had had a true change of heart. Swindlers, like gamblers, were addicted to the risks of the game. But...had Sayer sought out a woman who could aid and abet him with his nefarious plans? Her face was pretty enough to beguile an unsuspecting victim, and Miss Clayton had certainly been aware of her surroundings. A young lady raised in genteel circumstances would have walked blithely on, unaware she had been robbed, until she got to her destination. Had Sayer planned to add another accomplice?

She glanced around just then and Luke stepped into a recessed doorway to avoid being seen. He'd followed the hired hack from the train station to the general store, then remained at a discreet distance when she emerged and started walking. Now his intent was to see where she was going.

A female hand slid up his arm and, if he hadn't trained himself to have nerves of steel, he would have jumped out of his skin. He turned slowly to see a prostitute with too much paint on her face wink at him. Lord Almighty. How had *he* not noticed her approach?

"I dun't mind a cozy little space, gov." She moved closer and looked him up and down. "Although I must say *you* dun't need to be hidin' in corners. Yur a fine-lookin' one, you are."

"Thank you." He quickly sidestepped and moved onto the sidewalk. "But I don't have time for anything right now."

She fingered the lapel of his frockcoat. "Are you sure, gov?"

"Yes." He reached into his pocket for a coin to give to her. At least he still had his money. Hellfire. As intent as he'd been on following Miss Clayton, he wouldn't have been surprised if a pickpocket had gotten to him. "Here. Treat yourself to something."

The woman's eyes widened as she snatched the silver piece. "Thank you, gov. This here's my spot, if you change your mind. My name is Ruby." She winked again. "Just like my lips."

"Er…yes." From his peripheral vision, he could see Miss Clayton entering another hired hack. "I'll keep that in mind."

Not waiting for an answer, he strode across the street, climbed up to the bench beside a startled driver and tossed him a gold eagle. "Follow that carriage and don't lose it."

"Yes, sir!" The man snapped the reins sharply and his vehicle lurched into traffic.

It didn't take long before the first carriage slowed at a boarding house. Luke's driver looked at him. "Do you want me to stop?"

Luke shook his head. "Keep driving."

Now that he knew where she was staying, he would plan his own cover.

****

Her nape prickled as Abby stepped down from the carriage. She'd had the odd feeling she was being followed, but this neighborhood was much quieter and less trafficked. Only one carriage had passed, but it was already retreating in the distance. She shook her head to clear it. No doubt she was feeling leftover residue from the incident with the pickpockets. And she was rapidly growing aware of how fatigued she really was.

Paying the driver, she let herself through the wrought-iron gate. She stopped to look up at the boarding house. A rectangular wooden building three stories high, it had fresh white paint and green shutters. The graveled walkway to the varnished front door was bordered by tiny patches of neatly trimmed lawn on either side. The roof sloped upwards and flattened at the top, allowing for a small, square balcony of sorts, with wooden rails. Abby suspected there would be a spectacular view of the water from up there.

Compared to the crowded, dirty tenement in New York, it looked like a castle. And respectable. She was so glad John had steered her in this direction.

Abby hesitated at the door, wondering if she should knock, then decided since it was a boarding house there was no need. Turning the knob, she stepped through the door into a small foyer sparsely furnished with a small table, above which a mirror hung. A counter ran parallel near to one wall, with wooden pegs for keys and niches for mail behind it. Directly across was a small sitting room, and Abby moved toward it to peek inside. It was modestly furnished, but with comfortable-looking chairs. Down the short hall, she could hear the sounds of conversation as well as the clinking of tableware, so she assumed that was the public room where meals would be served.

"Can I help you?"

She turned at the sound. A woman with steel-gray hair and a no-nonsense expression stood behind the counter. Abby walked over to her. "Mrs. Bartlett?"

"That's me."

"I'd like to rent a room, if there's one available."

"You aren't one of them dance girls, are you?"

She couldn't help but smile. The only dancing she knew how to do was escaping from a mark. She sobered quickly. Her past was behind her. For good. "I am not a dancer. Mr. John…" She stopped, remembering she'd not gotten the man's last name. "The shopkeeper at Sayer's General Store suggested that you might let me a room."

One gray brow lifted. "Why would he do that?"

"I'm Abigail Clayton, Travis Sayer's mail-order bride. News of his sudden death didn't reach me before I left New York."

"Ah. He was a good tenant while he was here." Mrs. Bartlett's expression relaxed somewhat. "A senseless killing, from what I heard." She turned to her ledger. "How long will you be staying before you go back?"

"I don't plan to return East."

The woman looked up. "You don't?"

Abby shook her head. "I was married by proxy before I left, so now I'm Travis's widow. I intend to stay."

The woman regarded her for a moment. "There's not much work for a respectable woman in San Francisco. You'd be better off going back."

"I already told John that I intend to take over operations of the store."

Mrs. Bartlett's gaze sharpened. "You intend to run the store?"

"Yes. I think it will be quite exciting to learn the business."

"I see." The woman looked somewhat skeptical, then shrugged. "In that case, my husband and I will be glad to have you stay here."

"Thank you." Abby breathed a sigh of relief. For the first time, her life looked like it was turning around.

****

By the time Abby arrived at the general store early the second morning after her arrival, she felt a lot more confident in her undertaking. She'd spent most of yesterday morning in the law offices of Bermen and Bermen—solicitors recommended by Delia Blake, another widow who was staying at the boarding house—completing the legal paperwork that would make her the owner of her late husband's store. Or at least, the major owner. There was something in the deed about a silent partner entitled to twenty percent, but no name had been provided. Then she'd spent the afternoon shopping for several practical work dresses. Delia had wanted her to purchase a dinner gown as well, but she saw no reason for such a thing. At least not until she became a successful proprietress.

Determined to win John completely over to her side, she smoothed the skirt of her just-purchased calico, put a smile on her face, and stepped inside the store. And then stopped so abruptly she nearly toppled over despite her new half-boots.

The black-haired, black-clad man who'd been at the train station was standing by the counter.

John looked none too pleased, but the stranger smiled and gave her a short bow. "Mrs. Sayer?"

She blinked, then remembered that she was not Miss Clayton any longer. "Yes?"

"I'm Luke Cameron. Forgive me for not recognizing you at the train station, day before last."

Abby blinked again. "You were expecting me?"

The stranger inclined his head. "In a way. I knew Travis had contracted for a bride. I was expecting someone...a little older."

"I am two-and-twenty." She had always looked

younger than her age, an advantage when she would play the child who accidently stalled the person whose pocket her brother would pick. Then she frowned. "You knew Mr. Say…er, my husband?"

"We're cousins. I handle an investment syndicate. Travis had indicated that he wanted to expand his business here in San Francisco."

"I see. Well, I am now the owner of this store and obviously not ready to think about expanding it." Abby straightened, although her head barely came to his shoulder. Goodness, the man was tall and broad! She lifted her chin. "I'm not interested in selling, either."

Luke's unusual whiskey-colored eyes studied her before he nodded. "I'm not wanting to buy the store."

"Then that's settled." Abby gave a shaky sigh of relief, not quite sure why this stranger rattled her. "If you'll excuse me, I need to start getting to work."

"Of course. I'll be willing to help."

She started. "Help?"

He smiled again and removed a paper from the inside of his frockcoat. "Your husband signed a contract for the expansion before he was killed, and my investors agreed to the terms as well." He handed her the paper. "It seems we'll be partners, Mrs. Sayer."

Chapter Three

Luke observed Abigail Clayton-Sayer's reaction to his announcement. If he'd not had a gunslinger's keen sense for an adversary's slightest movement or shift in gaze, he might not have noticed the dilation that made her blue eyes suddenly look violet nor the quick, short intake of breath which made her breasts heave under the high-necked, proper cotton dress she wore. Her facial expression was as impassive as a poker player, and, coupling that with what he'd witnessed on the street two days before, he wondered again what her background was...and whether she was involved in Sayer's scams.

Beautiful women often turned out to be Jezebels. He should know.

And then there was the fact that she'd married-by-proxy *before* she came West. Most mail-order brides waited until they'd at least *seen* their future husbands before tying the knot. Had she known Sayer before? Had she known about his schemes and decided she wanted to make sure she got half of what he'd swindled?

That she planned to stay and run the store meant she was ambitious. Not that Luke could fault her for that, but how far did her ambition extend? Would she be willing to collude with Sayer's secret accomplice?

Time would tell.

But Hell's blazes! Did Abigail Clayton-Sayer have to be so damn alluring? Her face was devoid of paint, nor did cloyingly sweet perfume cling to her. He caught only the fresh scent of soap and perhaps a bit of rosewater wafting from her hair. Even in the prim, high-collared calico she wore, he could detect delicate curves in all the right places. Her golden hair was pulled back in a proper chignon, although a few tendrils had escaped, no doubt from the wind on her way over. His fingers itched to undo the pins and spread that golden halo with his hands as her sapphire eyes turned indigo with desire…

Luke gave himself an inward shake and refocused.

Right now, he had one foot in the door with his forged documents, thanks to a Pinkerton operative in San Francisco. He doubted Sayer ever had plans to expand. The store was probably just a cover to launder money. However, Luke's original plan of exposing the man's fraudulence to force him to sell the store and turn over the profits—if he didn't want to get the authorities involved—was no longer doable. Now he had to find the accomplice, which meant he needed to have a connection to the store.

"I'm sure you'll find the papers in order." Pinkerton operatives were nothing if not efficient.

She still looked a bit dazed as she glanced down at the paper. "Perhaps your investors might want to reconsider, given the change in circumstances."

"I suspect not." Since his grandmother and her friends hadn't been the only ones swindled, he'd managed to persuade the local Pinkerton office to grant him a bit of seed money to make the project look authentic. "San Francisco has increased its population by over two hundred percent since the Gold Rush began, and it's continuing to grow. That makes this town a lucrative investment."

"So why not just build another store and offer competition?"

The astuteness of her thinking shouldn't have surprised him, given the pickpocket scenario he'd witnessed. The question was logical, as well. "There are a number of general stores already providing competition. What makes this one stand out," he added before she could ask the next logical question, "is its location. There is still *room* for expansion. San Francisco is becoming a bit crowded anywhere near the bay."

She glanced around. "It seems to me that we have an excellent inventory. Why would adding to it be necessary?"

"It will be a different kind of inventory. More Eastern businessmen are relocating here, and they will want some refinements. My investors think to fill a need for the more luxurious items like imported tea. Exotic spices, too…cloves, cinnamon, nutmeg, ginger …and clothing dyes like red and indigo, as well as fine silks."

A corner of her mouth lifted along with a questioning arch of a brow. "Those items are more enticing to women than men."

"You are quite right, Mrs. Sayer." Luke paused. "A second part of the investment plan involves women."

The other brow went up. "How?"

"Wives accompany their husbands. They will want the luxuries they're accustomed to. That provides our market." He paused again. "It was suggested to the investors that another room could be added to the store. For now, though, we can clean out the storage area—"

"That's for our extra stock," John interrupted.

"The extra stock can be stored in the basement, can't it?" Luke asked. "That was another thing that made this building a good choice. It *has* a basement."

"But not fit for much," John countered. "Dirt floor and all."

"I can take a look at it."

"Never mind," John said quickly. "I suppose I can probably get pallets to keep things dry if I need to. But I don't see why we need more space for tea and spices."

Luke turned back to Abby. "We can refit the storage area into a sitting room of sorts, with comfortable furniture for these women to meet during the day to exchange pleasantries and sample the new products—"

"A women's club?" she asked, her tone skeptical.

"In a way, but I suspect women who are willing to travel West—such as yourself—are also somewhat independent-minded. My investors want to have local involvement ensuring that interest in the products continues." He lifted one shoulder, then let it drop. "I'll give them the opportunity to be a part of the expansion by using their household funds to invest independently of their husbands. For the first time, perhaps, they'll be able to make their own money. It will be small at first, but as the store profits grow, so will what they've contributed. I think that will appeal to many women."

Abigail considered. "I suppose it might."

Luke nodded. He also hoped it would appeal to the accomplice. When word got around that a women's club was organizing at Sayer's General Store to do investing, the bait would be too difficult to resist. He hoped.

"Until I have a chance to look over the accounts and see how much money is actually being made—"

"A good idea." Luke smiled at her and looked at the dour shopkeeper. "Perhaps John can show the books to both of us."

"I don't take care of those. Bronson did, and then Sayer." The man shoved a ledger across the counter. "Everything you need to know is in there."

Luke flipped it open. "This is a record of sales."

"That's what you need, isn't it?"

"Partly. We also need to see monthly financial statements going back a year. Profit and loss figures. Things like that."

"I never seen them. Besides, they're confidential."

Luke forced a patient smile. "I understand that, but I need to report back to my investors that the store is in financially strong standing."

"And since I'm the new owner, I need to see those records too," Abby said.

John looked from one to the other and then he shrugged. "I suppose they're in the back office."

"Will you show us?" Abby asked.

He gave a grudging nod and led them to the back of the store where he opened a door to a tiny room hardly big enough for the desk and two chairs in it.

Luke managed to repress a grin. He had intended to spend as long as it took to do a very thorough scouring of each entry and every account, but sharing this enclosed space with Abigail would warrant him taking even more time. Much more.

****

Even though John had left the door open, Abby was all too aware of the small space she shared with Luke Cameron. And all too aware of the man himself. Although he was obviously educated and spoke like a gentleman, everything else about him exuded pure animal strength and magnetism, from his wolf-colored eyes to his black hair that was just a bit too longish and the dark shadow that was already forming along his strong jaw. He moved with the same litheness of feral cats who stalked rats in the allies of New York. And, dressed in black as he was, he reminded her of a panther she'd seen once in a cage in a travelling show. The animal had looked dangerous.

A little shiver slid down her spine.

"Perhaps it's best if we sit next to each other," Luke said as he pulled the second chair behind the desk. "So we can both look at the accounts."

"I don't think there's enough room there." *Criminy.* That sounded really stupid. "I mean, I think I'll be able to see from the side." That sounded even more stupid.

A corner of his mouth lifted. "I won't bite. I promise."

She felt her face heat. Of course, he wouldn't *bite*. But looking at his wide, full mouth curled in a lazy half-smile made her suddenly wonder what it would feel like to have his lips on hers. *Criminy crickets!* Where had that thought come from? Since she'd first grown to womanhood, she'd avoided men who wanted kisses. Her mother had warned her that allowing that kind of liberty only led to trouble.

And now it felt like a tiny devil sat on her shoulder, prodding her with his pitchfork. *Maybe it wouldn't be so bad.* She chanced a look at her shoulder just to make sure it was empty. Silly her. She took a deep breath and went around the desk to perch on the edge of the chair.

Luke watched her movement, one brow arched ever so slightly, but he said nothing as he sat down as well and opened the first ledger John had shown them.

'We might as well start by looking at what's been selling in the store," he said. "Have you experience in managing accounts?"

Abby shook her head and looked at the neat rows of items and prices. "I can do sums, though."

"That's a beginning then."

Several hours later, she realized just how much of a "beginning" doing sums was. The desk was littered with monthly statements of costs and expenses, lists of inventory and vendors, invoices, and a calendar with delivery schedules. Luke seemed to have no difficulty understanding any of it. In fact, he'd dug into one ledger after another with the ferocity of those feral alley cats at a rat hole.

She certainly didn't need to worry about him *biting* her. He'd hardly paid any attention to her at all. Which was probably just as well, considering how truly naïve she was about running a business. It would not do to have him—or John—find out. She would just have to come back after hours when no one was here and figure things out for herself.

Because she was going to make this work.

She had to.

****

The slight stirring at his side made Luke divert his attention from the paperwork he'd strewn over the desk. Abigail had sat still as a statue while he'd stacked the various documents according to category. He'd never known any woman to be silent as long as she had been. He didn't know they *could* be. He'd asked her if she minded him separating and sorting the accounts first before they went through them, and she'd nodded her assent. Since then, she hadn't said a word. It was a bit uncanny.

"What would you like to go over first?" he asked.

Abigail glanced over the paper-covered desk. "I'm not sure. Where would you suggest?"

"An actual count of the inventory will have to be taken, which can happen when the storage area is cleared out, but it seems there is enough supply on hand to meet demand." He sifted through a small stack of papers and took one out. "This is last month's Profit and Loss Statement. It appears the store is financially sound."

She gave him a spontaneous smile, one which was natural and without guile and made more endearing by a dimple in one cheek, and nodded. "That is good news."

"Yes." Luke wasn't ready to tell her at this time that the profit margin over the past year might have been just a little *too* good. Running well over fifteen percent each month made him think the money credited to the assets side may not have come *only* from the general items sold. It smacked of money being laundered...funneled into a legitimate business only a little at a time so as not to create suspicion. It would be easy enough to slip in additional fake sales receipts. He needed to check those against actual inventory. "My investors will be pleased to hear this."

"And your investors won't expect me to use my profits to fund your imports?"

"No." It was a shrewd question for her to ask and he was glad she did. "We will make the initial investment of the tea and spices, but the goal is to make those items pay for themselves through the ladies' investment club, which will also further expand the business." He gave her a reassuring look. "I don't expect you to use any of your money until the endeavor can be proved worthwhile."

If what Luke suspected was true, he didn't want

Abigail to have *any* kind of connection to the bogus investment club. He was setting it up strictly to flush out Sayer's accomplice. Once he'd accomplished that—and consequently forced the sale of the store, if necessary—whatever money those ladies contributed to the club would be returned.

Although his career with Pinkerton's mainly involved using his six-shooter "peace-maker" to persuade criminals to see the light—either here in this world or beyond—he'd dealt with enough sham covers to know how they worked. He'd unearth the crook who'd gone to ground and get back the money his grandmother and her elderly friends had lost.

He just needed to keep Abigail Clayton-Sayer out of the fray.

Chapter Four

"Allow me to drive you home," Luke said as they walked out of the store later that afternoon.

Abby looked up and down the empty street. "I don't see a carriage waiting."

"There's a stable one block over. I keep a buggy there."

"Do you live near here then?"

He shook his head. "I stay at the Occidental Hotel over on Montgomery Street."

Even though she'd only been in San Francisco a short time, she knew the Occidental was a really expensive hotel. But of course, someone who handled investments would stay in a place like that. "That's in the opposite direction of my boarding house. I wouldn't want to put you to the trouble."

"No trouble. You'd have to walk all the way to Jackson Square to hire a hack."

She didn't want to tell him that after the first day, when she'd done just that, she realized they cost too much...at least for now, until she had some inkling of what kind of money she was really making. The numbers on all those papers they'd looked at had been confusing. She didn't relish walking the near mile to the boarding house. "Well, if you're sure..."

He smiled. "I'm sure."

They spoke of trifling things like the weather on the

short walk to the stables. Abby noticed that Luke walked next to the curb, keeping her to the inside of the earthen pathway that ran alongside the cobblestone street. She'd seen gentlemen walking their ladies like that in New York—Ben always preferred the man be walking to the lady's left because it made it easier to snatch her reticule and run—but Abby had never experienced such proper manners herself. No man had ever courted her, and when she walked beside Ben, it was as a lookout for a likely target, not because she might get mud on her skirts. Abby frowned. She had to stop thinking of the past. It was *over*.

"Are your feet sore?" Luke asked. "I should have offered to bring the buggy around."

For a moment she stared at him, uncomprehending. He thought her feet were sore? From walking a block? She wasn't sure if he was just being a gentleman again— it was kind of a *nice* thought—or if he thought she was really that delicate. Being thought fragile wouldn't do at all. Not if she was going to be a businesswoman. "I can assure you I've walked miles before without sore feet."

One dark brow rose slightly. "I thought New York had hacks everywhere."

"Not in the Bowery," she replied and then could have bitten her tongue off. She could only hope Luke wasn't familiar with the city and didn't know the kind of conditions the area had. "I mean…it was sometimes just quicker to walk."

"I see." Luke gestured as they arrived at the stable. "You won't have to walk today."

Abby felt her eyes widen as a groomsman led out a beautiful animal whose black coat glistened nearly blue in the sunshine. From the well-formed head with intelligent eyes to the flowing mane and tail, even she knew it was pure-blooded. She didn't need anyone to tell her it was a stallion, either. That was obvious from the way the horse pranced in his traces and tossed his head. His actions reminded her of Luke.

"This is Diablo," he said as he ran a hand over the horse's arched neck as it snorted.

"He's beautiful."

"Let him get to know you," Luke said. "Come closer."

He'd lowered his voice and it sounded seductive. Surely he didn't mean… *Criminy.* He didn't mean come closer to *him.* He meant the horse. That's why he was talking in that voice, too. It seemed to calm the animal. The tone had a rather opposite effect on her.

She walked toward the horse and held out her hand like she had to make friends with the mongrel dogs that roamed the Bowery's alleys. She wasn't sure it would work with horses, though, and this one certainly wasn't a mongrel. To her surprise, he nuzzled her hand.

"His nose feels like velvet."

"It's a muzzle," Luke said and smiled. "He likes you."

She felt inordinately pleased at the compliment. "I like him, too. Why did you name him Diablo? Doesn't that mean 'devil' in Spanish?" She'd heard the dialect—and word—spoken by immigrants on New York streets from the West Indies.

"It does." Luke stroked the horse's neck again. "I came across him at a rodeo in Wyoming a few years back."

"A rodeo?" Abby had never seen one, but she'd heard stories of the Wild West. "I thought they used wild horses. Diablo looks like some of the horses in Central

Park…like he came from fine English stock."

"Belgium. He's a Friesian." Luke shrugged. "A rancher wanted to use him to start a new breeding line, but he couldn't be broken to saddle so the man sold him to the rodeo circuit."

"And you rescued him?"

For a moment, Luke's expression changed and became introspective, then he smiled. "You might say he rescued me. Those were low times."

Abby felt a sudden empathy. It was hard to imagine Luke having low times, but she knew from experience that people didn't always get to choose their fate. "I've had some low times too." Then, before he could ask her what she meant, she changed the subject. "So you only use Diablo for harness? You don't ride him?"

Luke smiled again. "He lets me ride him."

Abby looked at the horse and then back at Luke. "How did you get him to accept a saddle if he wouldn't before?"

"I think we're kindred spirits." His smile faded. "I never tried to break him and he didn't try to break me." Then it was his turn to change the subject. "Shall we go?"

As she stepped into the buggy, Abby had a feeling there was a whole lot of Luke Cameron that lay well hidden beneath the surface of an educated gentleman.

****

"Who in the world was that absolutely devastating man?"

Delia had hardly given Abby a chance to step inside the foyer of the boarding house before she asked the question. Luke had walked her to the door, opened it, and given her a short bow before returning to his carriage. From the way Delia was bouncing on her toes to look out the side pane beside the door as the buggy drove away, Abby suspected she was a lot more than just curious.

Which annoyed her for no reason.

"That was my late husband's cousin, Luke Cameron."

Delia sighed and settled back on her heels. "He sure doesn't look anything like Mr. Sayer."

Her conscience niggled at her. Other than the description Travis had given her of himself, she hadn't really thought about what he looked like. She hadn't thought whether his features were regular or flawed. On the other hand, Luke Cameron's face was permanently etched into her brain. Not just the unusual wolf-colored eyes, but his high cheekbones, a slightly crooked nose that had probably been broken at some point, the wide, full mouth that she'd spent far too much time looking at this afternoon, and the firm jaw that seemed to be perpetually shadowed with stubble.

"I didn't realize you knew my…Travis."

"Just about every woman around here did." Delia clapped a hand over her mouth. "I didn't mean for it to sound like that."

Abby raised a brow and walked into the sitting room to avoid their conversation being heard by Mrs. Bartlett at the counter. After what the young man at the train station had said, she wasn't particularly surprised at Delia's remark. Evidently, her new—and newly departed—husband had been something of a rounder. "It's all right," she said once she and Delia were seated near the unlit hearth. "It's not like I got to know him."

"Well, he was right charmin'." Delia clapped her mouth shut again. "He did stay here for a short time before he moved to fancier digs."

"You don't have to explain," Abby said.

"Yes, I do. It weren't like he ever asked a lady out to dinner or anything," Delia replied. "Least not that I knew of."

That might explain why he had been with a saloon girl, although from the account, it didn't appear he'd been trying to charm the woman.

Delia went on. "Because of the gold mine tunnel that collapsed a few months ago, there's a bunch of us who're newly widowed. Mr. Sayer called on each of us and offered a discount at his store."

At least that was something positive. "Did he mention anything about expanding the store?"

"Didn't say. Why?"

"His cousin—Mr. Cameron—has a letter that says Travis planned to expand the store. He has some investors that are interested in the project."

"Oooh!" Delia grinned widely. "And you'll get to work with him?"

Abby wasn't sure how successful she'd be at that, considering she'd spent hours practically ogling the man and not paying attention to much else. Although, in her defense, she didn't understand what all those pieces of paper were. And it wasn't her fault either that Luke Cameron had the looks of one of those roguish men on the covers of those dime novels she used to pick out of the garbage.

She gave herself a mental shake. She was a newly-minted businesswoman. She *would* work with the man. And she would *concentrate* on business. "I suppose." She really needed to sound like she knew what she was doing, if only to prove the point to herself. "I'll have to look into the account books and make sure Travis was making enough of a profit for expanding the store to pay off."

"Mr. Sayer did sound right smart," Delia said. "He offered to help us straighten out any debts or bills we didn't understand." She gave Abby a bright smile. "That was right kind of him, wasn't it?"

She supposed it was. "Did anyone take him up on it?"

"I don't rightly know that there was time. He got... Well, there was the accident."

The one that made her a widow too. Abby wasn't sure how much of the details Delia actually knew, but perhaps it was best not to ask. "The shopkeeper said he'd written me about that, but the letter must have arrived after I'd already started out."

"You'll have to meet the other widows soon," Delia said. "Those of us who aren't looking to marry again right away kind of band together."

An idea struck Abby. Perhaps those other widowed ladies might be interested in the kind of club Luke wanted to start. She'd have to tell him about them. She smiled at her friend. "I'd like that."

****

It was late when Abby returned to the store that night. She had to wait until the public room had shut down and those residing at the boarding house had retired to their rooms. She was pretty sure if Delia—or possibly even Mrs. Bartlett—had known she planned to go out this late they would have insisted she take a hack, which right now she couldn't afford. She and Ben had spent enough time on the streets in the Bowery that she'd learned certain tricks to avoid being accosted. Besides, she had a set of Ben's clothes she could use to disguise that she was woman.

She let herself into the store with the key she'd purloined from the peg on the wall earlier that day. "Purloined" probably was not the correct word, since she owned the store, but John hadn't offered a key. Since she didn't want to be antagonistic by reminding him that he was, literally, in her employ now, she felt it easier simply to lift the extra key.

The streetlight shone through the front display window, allowing her to avoid hitting any of the barrels or boxes of merchandise on her way to the small office in the back. Once inside, she lit a small oil lamp, closed the door, and sat down at the desk. Luke had left the papers in neat little stacks beside the sales ledger. She put the lists of inventory aside. She could count, for goodness' sake, and they'd be going over that when they cleaned out the storage unit, probably tomorrow. The schedules for delivery were fairly clear, as well, although when she got to the actual accounting book with its complicated entries of debits and credits, she had to slow down. Accounts Receivable and Accounts Payable were new terms. What seemed to her should have been a credit was actually listed as a debit and the numbers in the other column were considered a credit. She was going to have to ponder on that.

The oil in the lamp was nearly gone by the time she leaned back and rubbed her eyes. Her mind was swimming with what were assets and what were liabilities such as expenses for wages, maintenance and office supplies, and repairs. There was a lot more to running a business than simply having items to sell. From what she could make out of the Profit and Loss Statement—she'd have to ponder on that more closely too—was that the store was making enough money to have a solid footing. She wouldn't become wealthy, although if Luke Cameron's investors were correct, that might happen in the future. For now, she wasn't about to get greedy.

Abby doused the lamp as she opened the office door and made her way through the store. She was about to leave when she heard a noise outside. Standing stock-still, she tuned her ears. What sounded like shuffling and then a heavy thud came from outside the store to the right. Making her way to the window but staying in its shadow, she looked out—and what she saw widened her eyes.

John and another man were rolling what appeared to be a barrel toward the street, where a buckboard waited. She hadn't even heard it arrive, but then she'd been in the back with the door closed. As she watched, they hefted it onto the back where one barrel already stood. They disappeared around the corner of the store only to reappear a few minutes later with another barrel. Abby remembered now that the cellar below was only accessible from the outside. She'd nearly tripped over the door that lay flat on the ground like a lid on a jar when she'd walked around the property earlier. The door had been nearly hidden by shrubbery overgrowth and had a stout lock on it.

So what on earth were the men doing? She watched as the two men made several more trips, bringing more barrels out before climbing onto the buckboard and driving off.

Abby let herself out of the store and mulled the situation as she started walking in the opposite direction toward the boarding house. John had said the cellar wasn't good for much since it had dirt floors, although Luke had said they could put in wood pallets for the inventory they were going to remove from the storage room. Maybe John had enlisted a friend to help him clear out old barrels that had been left to rot down there. Maybe he wanted to have the cellar cleaned out and be ready for the inventory tomorrow. That would account for why he was doing it in the middle of the night. Although, from the lavender tint to the sky, dawn was not that far away. She'd have to hurry to be back in her room before others started waking up.

Still, it spoke well of John that he would give up his sleep to impress her—or at least, Luke—with the semblance of a clean cellar for the inventory. He no doubt wanted to keep his position. Which was fine with her.

Perhaps one day, he'd be as loyal to her as he obviously was to Travis.

Chapter Five

John was already at the store when Abby arrived the next morning. Granted, she had slept in a little later than usual since she'd gotten home barely before dawn, but then John had been up most of the night as well. She had no idea how much junk had been in the cellar or how many wagonloads he'd had to remove. She'd only spotted the buckboard when she'd been ready to leave.

She was tempted to tell him thanks, but she didn't really want anyone to know she'd been there looking over the accounts. Besides, Luke had already arrived and she certainly did not want him knowing how intimidating the books were.

He wore Levis and a blue chambray shirt today instead of his usual black attire, although he still had his six-gun strapped to his thigh. A muscular thigh that the tight denims did nothing to hide. Strange how the change of clothes seemed to change him. In his gentleman's dark frock and waistcoats, she could easily picture him at one of the gaming hells, presiding over a game of poker. Today, he looked more like the cowboys she'd seen at the train stops on this side of the Mississippi River. She glanced down. He was even wearing brown leather boots with hand tooling on the sides like the cowboys favored.

It looked like he was dressed to work instead of supervise. Somehow, that idea pleased her. "Are we ready to start moving the inventory out of the storage area?"

"In just a bit," Luke answered. "I ordered wood pallets for the floor. The lumberyard said they'd deliver first thing this morning." He turned to John. "Is there anything that needs to be cleared out down there while we wait?"

The man shook his head. Abby wondered why he didn't mention he'd worked last night to clean it out, but maybe he didn't want to sound like he was fishing for a compliment. Men had their pride, especially when they were talking to other men.

"Nothin' down there." John glanced at her. "Except some rats and maybe a snake or two."

Was he trying to intimidate her? It wasn't like she hadn't seen huge sewer rats in the alleys of the Bowery. And other vermin going through the garbage, as well. Of course, he wouldn't know that, since Travis had thought he was getting a gently bred, educated lady who'd recently fallen on hard times and been left to fend for herself in the world. Well, at least the last half of her concocted story was true.

Obviously, she had not won John completely over to the idea of her running the store. Abby forced a benign expression. "I'm sure once we start moving things in down there, they'll retreat to safer territory."

"More likely they'll start eating holes in the burlap bags to get at the victuals." He looked at Luke. "Better to keep everything up here in the storage area."

"That would require my investors to put up money to build an extension," Luke replied.

"Isn't that what you—they—wanted?" John retorted.

"Eventually, perhaps. It depends on how successful

we are with the initial proposal." Luke gestured in her direction. "I'm sure Mrs. Sayer doesn't want to invest her capital on a venture at this point either."

"No, I don't." From what she'd been able to make out—if she understood the paperwork she'd gone through last night—the profit margin was large enough to fund building, but she wasn't going to take the risk. "Using the storage area for a tea room of sorts will give us an idea if the plan will work."

Luke nodded. "Besides, I asked the lumberyard to bring some enclosed crates, also. Anything that can be gnawed at will be placed in those."

Abby gave him a genuine smile. "That was thoughtful of you."

"Pragmatic," he answered. "Inventory lost is profit lost."

They were interrupted by the sound of horses' hooves and creaking wagon wheels approaching. "That must be your order," she said.

"And on time," Luke replied.

For the next thirty minutes, Abby watched as Luke supervised the men unloading the wagon and then disappeared into the cellar along with John. She'd wanted to help but quickly realized she was more in the way while the men carried the unwieldy heavy pallets down the stone steps and then lugged the big wooden crates down after that.

However, once that had been done and the wagon was gone, she stepped into the storage room and began removing items she could carry down. Luke stopped her.

"It's dusty down there. You'll ruin your clothes."

It wasn't like she'd not gotten dirty before. She and Ben had had to hide in some rather nasty places sometimes to evade getting caught. But John wasn't the only one to think she came from at least a respectable Eastern background. Luke thought her proper, too.

"I can't just stand around while you do all the work."

He handed her the list of inventory that had been lying on the office desk the night before. "You can help by checking off the items as I take them down."

"I'll probably need to be down there too so I can see where everything goes." John spoke up suddenly. "So she can run the counter too."

Abby was glad the shopkeeper had volunteered his services. "Of course! I'll be glad to. Thank you for helping."

He shrugged. "Seein' as how I'll be the one goin' down there to fetch things, it'll be easier if I know where everything is."

"Makes sense," Luke said. "Let's get started then."

It was late afternoon by the time they'd finally cleared everything out of the storage room. It looked vastly bigger when empty than it had before.

"I think we can probably fit two sofas in here, along with several armchairs and a few small tables," Abby said to Luke as they stood in the doorway.

He grinned, his teeth flashing white as he wiped dirt off his face with a rag. "You can start furnishing the place tomorrow. How about if I get cleaned up and take you to dinner?"

Her pulse quickened and what felt like a dozen butterflies fluttered in her stomach. No one had ever asked her to a meal before. "Dinner? Just us?" As soon as the words came out, she wanted to push them back into her mouth. What a stupid thing to say.

He studied her before he answered. "We'll be in the

public room at the Occidental Hotel."

Criminy. Did he think she was afraid to be alone with him? She wasn't, although her skin tingled a bit like it used to before she and Ben pulled a heist. And maybe her breath became a bit more shallow…

"I want to discuss how we're going to handle this new enterprise," he added.

That statement dissolved any kind of anticipation she might have been feeling. "Ah…yes. That's a good idea."

Of course he wasn't interested in her company for dinner. He wanted to talk business. They would be working together after all.

It would behoove her to remember that.

****

"I don't care what you say." Delia framed a few loose hair strands around Abby's face. "If the man's taking you to dinner, he has courting on his mind."

Abby rolled her eyes as she sat on the small bench in front of an equally small dressing table in Delia's room, and she pulled her wrapper tighter. She would have tried to stand, but Delia had already pushed her down twice while admonishing her to be still so she could fix Abby's hair. "*He* is the one who said he wanted to discuss business."

"Hogwash." Delia plucked another curl loose. "What a man says is not always what he means."

"There's not much room for misinterpretation," Abby replied. "He wants to talk about how we're going to handle this women's club thing."

"Aha! He said *we*," Delia pounced on the word. "As in *you and him*."

She started to shake her head, then stopped as her

hair got pulled since Delia was still fiddling with it. "Since I own the store and Travis arranged for a group of investors to expand, Luke has to work with me."

"Aha!" Delia said again. "You called him *Luke*."

Abby sighed since she couldn't move her head. "It's a little silly to call him Mr. Cameron when he's been doing manual labor all day, hauling the inventory down to the cellar."

"Um. There's nothing like a man sweating and toiling and showing off his muscles," Delia said.

Abby started to reply, then closed her mouth. She couldn't deny that was true. She had—unobtrusively while she was checking off items, of course—watched him bend, lift, and carry. The exertion soon had the cotton chambray shirt clinging to him, molding beautifully broad shoulders and strong back muscles as well as bulging biceps. And the Levis fit like a second skin too. Men in New York favored pantaloons and some still wore knee breeches. Neither revealed nearly half what these blue denim creations did. It was a wonder Western women got any work done. Or maybe it was just the way Luke wore them. His black attire fit him equally well.

"There." Delia finished her fussing with Abby's hair. "That should do it."

Abby glanced at herself in the little mirror above the dressing table. Delia had arranged most of her hair on top of her head in a swirl of curls, with a few ringlets dangling down over one shoulder. The effect made her look like a real lady.

"And now this." Delia returned from her wardrobe and held up a deep blue silk gown. "Thank goodness we're about the same size."

"I can't wear that."

"Why not? It will bring out the color of your eyes."

"I don't think Luke—Mr. Cameron—is interested in the color of my eyes."

"Fiddlesticks." Delia removed the gown from its hanger. "He'll get lost in the depths of them."

Abby looked heavenward. "I doubt very much that he's the type to wax poetic about the color of my eyes. He's more interested in the color of money."

"Balderdash. He'll forget all about gold, silver, or greenbacks once he gets a glimpse of you."

A sound escaped her, something between a snort and a laugh. "I told you. Luke—Mr. Cameron—wants to discuss *business*."

Delia waved a dismissive hand. "He may *think* he does. He'll change his mind once he sees you in this. Besides," she said when Abby still hesitated, "what else do you have to wear that would be suitable for the Occidental? It's a fancy hotel."

There was that. Other than her traveling outfit—which still needed cleaning—the rest of her clothing, including the new things she'd bought, were serviceable and plain. She was going to be nervous enough trying to remember which piece of silverware to use first. Her only etiquette lessons had come from the Sisters of Mercy, and they didn't use a bunch of forks and spoons, to say nothing of crystal goblets and real china. With that to worry about, she didn't need to draw any more attention to herself by wearing a work dress.

"All right. Just this once."

"I have another gown you can wear next time," Delia said, as though she hadn't heard, and pulled the wrapper's ties loose.

"There's not going to be a next time." Abby's words were muffled as Delia carefully started placing the gown over her head. "This is *business*."

"If you say so," Delia said cheerfully.

She was proving very efficient as a lady's maid. In less than five minutes, she had the gown laced—a bit too tightly for Abby's comfort—and had shaken out the folds of the skirt. Then she tugged the neckline a bit lower. Abby tugged it back up. "I'm not trying to seduce the man."

Delia grinned. "Doesn't hurt to try."

"Will you stop?"

"Oh, all right." She puffed up the short sleeves on the gown. "He'll take notice anyway. The color suits you. It really does."

Abby refrained from grimacing. Obviously her friend was hell-bent on romance blooming. "He's not going to get lost in the color of my eyes."

Undeterred, Delia shrugged. "We'll see."

****

He was lost in the color of her eyes. Luke looked across the table in the Occidental's dining room and wondered what kind of witchery was this. The Abigail Clayton he'd seen at the train station had looked entrancing and a bit vulnerable. The Mrs. Sayer at the store today had been completely proper. Even a little prim in her high-necked, long-sleeved calico. But the woman who was sitting across from him tonight was a siren. The gown was the same color as the deep blue of the bay and brought out the sapphire in her eyes. And she'd done something with her hair. The burnished gold curls piled high were loose enough to make a man wonder... If he pulled out just one pin, would all of it cascade down past her shoulders and touch the swell of her breasts? The tops of which were just visible at the neckline of her bodice. A bodice that left no room for *imagining* what curves lay behind it.

And, damn it, he knew better than to fall for an attractive woman. Belle Fontaine had been beautiful, too.

Belle, whose name meant "beauty" and whose heart was black as coal. A friendly competition had begun two years ago between him and his best friend Karl when Belle—the famous singer at the world-renowned Southern Hotel in St. Louis—started flirtations with both of them. The competition turned deadly after she'd secretly declared to each of them that the other had defiled her. She had been mightily persuasive, with crocodile tears and bruises marring her milky-white wrists. They'd both been taken for fools, and after their duel she'd moved on to a gent far wealthier.

If there was any redeeming quality to the whole sordid incident, it was that Karl's twin brother Kelvin had been working for the U.S. ambassador in London for the past two years. Otherwise, more than one person might be dead, since he was as hot-headed as Karl had been.

"Is something wrong?" Abby asked.

Luke blinked, bringing the woman presently at the table into focus. It was unfair to make such a comparison between the two women. He knew that. But what the deuce was Abigail trying to do? "Nothing wrong. I was wool-gathering."

"You must have spotted a wolf among your sheep."

He frowned. "What?"

"Sorry. I was trying to make a jest of your *wool*-gathering." She shrugged. "Your eyes flashed as though you were angry about something."

He was slipping if he'd let any emotion show. Gunslingers and card sharks—he had experience with both—never let their opponents know what was going on inside their heads. Was Abigail that intuitive? Or did she have a hidden past like he did? He recalled the incident with the pickpocket. She'd sensed and actually caught the street urchin. Not many people would be able to do that.

Supposedly she'd come West as a mail-order bride, but she'd quickly decided to run the general store and had, indeed, shown an aptitude for understanding business. Luke didn't think she was the accomplice he was looking for, since all the information he'd gathered through Pinkerton pointed to a male, but perhaps she'd come West to launch a new scheme with Sayer?

He'd have to play his hand carefully.

The waiter appeared, intent on removing their first course of turtle soup and replacing it with fillet of salmon covered with creamed curry sauce and accompanied by new red potatoes and roasted squash. Abby closed her eyes and inhaled the delicious aromas.

"This has got to be the best dinner I've ever had."

He refrained from smiling at the way she heartily dug into the food. She'd scraped her soup bowl clean, too. He appreciated a woman with a healthy appetite—it usually meant they had a healthy appetite in bed as well…which he shouldn't be thinking about—but he wondered about her somewhat limited comportment.

He poured her a second glass of wine. "Be sure to save room for dessert. The cherry tarts here are excellent."

"Mmmm," she said, scooping up some sauce with

her spoon. "That sounds good."

When he'd questioned John earlier, the man said Travis had told him his mail-order bride was a well-educated, refined lady who'd been orphaned. That didn't match up with her behavior this evening. Although she'd been subtle, he'd noticed her gazing around the dining room with its white linen tablecloths and sparkling crystal chandeliers. That probably was not too surprising. Many people were awed at such opulence in a hotel this far West, but he'd sensed she didn't feel at ease. She'd hesitated, too, in selecting appropriate silverware, furtively watching him and then following his lead. Again, he wondered about her past.

"You said you wanted to discuss business," Abigail said as the waiter brought desserts. "Yet you haven't mentioned it once."

That's because he couldn't concentrate on the general store at the moment, all too aware of the ravishing beauty across from him. He apparently had not learned his lesson from Belle Fontaine after all.

"Perhaps it can wait." He needed to find out more information about this puzzling lady before he laid out his cards. "My apologies. My grandmother always told me it was rude to discuss business at dinner anyway."

Abby looked up from her tart to inquire, "Your grandmother?"

"Yes. She raised me when my parents were killed in a carriage accident in St. Louis years ago." Luke watched her face covertly for any sign that she knew of Travis' scam to divest the elderly of their money. All he saw, though, was sympathy.

"I'm sorry. My mother died a couple of years ago."

That coincided with what John had told him. "And

your father?"

A muscle ticked in her cheek, barely noticeable. "I never knew my father."

Luke wanted to ask why, but her expression—and his grandmother's voice inside his head admonishing him to mind his manners—made him refrain. "That must have been difficult."

"We managed. I am here now." Picking up her wine glass, she smiled, although it looked forced. "To new adventures."

"To new adventures." As he lifted his glass, his eyes were on her mouth, her lips a lush pink from the wine. He felt himself harden.

Damn it. He needed to be concentrating on finding out who she really was, not how she'd taste if he kissed her.

Chapter Six

"So how did dinner go last night?" Delia asked Abby the next morning as they met in the public room for breakfast.

"The hotel's dining room was lovely." Abby scooped scrambled eggs onto her plate from the sideboard, added a slice of ham as well as a biscuit, and looked around. Since it was a Sunday morning, the room was pretty much empty, but she headed for a table in the corner to ensure privacy. From the look on Delia's face, she was going to want a full account.

Her friend had hardly seated herself before she asked, "Did you discuss *business*?"

"No, actually we didn't—"

"Aha! I knew it! He just used that as a ruse."

"I don't think—"

"Here's what *I* think." Delia smirked. "The man is planning to court you."

"Don't be silly. We're going to be business partners."

"Which is *why* he said he wanted to discuss *business*." Delia gave her a sly wink. "I think monkey business is more like it."

"He didn't mention a monkey at all."

Delia rolled her eyes. "You know very well what I mean."

She wasn't really sure that she did. The Sisters of

52

Mercy did not encourage any kind of interaction with boys. She and Ben had even been separated into different rooms for their reading and writing lessons. Suggestions from men on the streets were not anything she wished to entertain. Basically, she had no experience in the art of flirtation.

"Luke—Mr. Cameron—said it was rude to discuss business at dinner. He even apologized for bringing it up."

"Proves my point," Delia said with a self-satisfied smile.

"Does it?" She couldn't recall Luke giving her any compliments. If he were attempting to flirt, wouldn't he have at least told she looked nice in the blue gown? He had certainly given it more than a passing glance. But then his expression had changed. She'd caught what looked like a flash of anger in his eyes, but it passed so quickly she wasn't sure that's what it was. But then, he had appeared almost melancholy for another fleeting moment. She was pretty sure neither of those expressions lent themselves to flirtation. After that, their conversation had been superficial and he'd been the perfect gentleman on the short ride back to the boarding house.

"Yes, it does. Did he sit next to you in the carriage? Did his leg brush yours? Did he linger over saying goodbye?" Delia asked. "Or did he maybe try to steal a kiss?"

Abby felt her face heat out of embarrassment. "None of those things happened."

"Ummm." Delia took a sip of coffee. "Well, that just proves he's a gentleman."

"That's what I tried to tell you."

Delia grinned. "Just wait until next time, though."

"You're incorrigible." Not that she wasn't just the teeniest bit disappointed. Luke had dressed in all-black attire again and looked magnificent. With his dark hair brushing his collar, along with the shadow of beard and his golden wolf-eyes, more than one lady's head had turned when they'd walked into the room. But there was also a virility and intensity about him that drew Abby in as if this man would stop at nothing to protect someone he loved.

Not that she was thinking about love. She just wondered what it would feel like to have such a champion. To know that she was utterly and completely safe from the harsh reality of the world. She'd also wondered—if she wanted to be completely truthful with herself—what it would be like to have such a man kiss her. Probably not safe at all, if the strange fluttering in her stomach was an indication.

But it was a moot point. Luke had not even kissed her gloved hand. At any rate, it was definitely time to change the subject.

"Perhaps it was best we didn't discuss business after all," she said. "I had planned to tell Luke—Mr. Cameron—about the widowed ladies you mentioned Travis had called upon, but maybe it was better I didn't."

"Why not?" Delia asked. "They'd be a perfect group to start your ladies' club or whatever you call it."

"I agree," Abby said, "but I think if it's going to be a ladies' group that also might want to invest, we should issue specific invitations asking them to attend a special opening once the tea imports arrive."

Delia shrugged. "They'll probably jump at the chance to sample tea and meet. There isn't much of a social life for widows here."

"That may be, but I think they should know the potential for them to become businesswomen—sort of—in their own right." Abby buttered her biscuit. "That way, they won't think we tricked them in any way."

Delia nodded. "That's true."

"It would be a good way to ensure there's good attendance, too. And…" Abby took a bite, chewed and swallowed as she thought. "It'll be a surprise for Mr. Cameron if the ladies who show up already know why they're there."

Delia gave her a side glance along with another grin. "And, maybe out of gratitude, *Mr. Cameron* will take you to dinner again?"

"You really are incorrigible." But Abby felt her face warm again, not from embarrassment this time, but from anticipation.

Maybe he would.

****

Luke poured himself a healthy dose of brandy from the decanter on the small table beside the window of the room he was renting. Tossing it back in one swoop, he watched the sun setting over the bay, just as he had every evening for the last two weeks, as he waited for the shipment of tea and silks he'd ordered. The *Neptune Maiden* was due in any day now. Meanwhile, he'd tried not to think of the evening he'd had dinner with Abigail. Fortunately—or not, depending on his mood—Abigail had maintained a strictly businesslike attitude with him since then.

For someone who needed nerves of steel to shoot fast and straight, he was unnerved by her, and he suspected it wasn't just because, dressed as she was that night, she'd reminded him of Belle.

He'd been in Abigail's presence nearly a month and he knew she was nothing like the Jezebel who'd forced two friends into a duel where one of them ended up dead. Abigail was kind and not at all vain. Fortunately—or not, depending on his mood—she'd not flirted with him at all. For all of her physical beauty, he had the odd sense that she didn't wish to call that kind of attention to herself. Which made him wonder why.

In his experience, most unencumbered women, even those not nearly so comely, vied for attention. A few, like Belle, craved power and wealth in their own right. Others simply wanted compliments and pretty words, and some prowled with the parson's noose wrapped up in their reticules. He'd always quickly sidestepped those, preferring widows who had no desire to remarry.

Abigail was a widow, albeit it a virginal one. Damn it all, he'd like to show her some bed sport. The paradox intrigued him. Then again, maybe it wasn't a paradox. If she had met Travis before and decided to become a partner in his scams, she might very well have consummated her marriage-by-proxy before she came West. That would make more sense than legally marrying a man before meeting him, at least.

Something was off about the whole situation. He didn't know what it was, but his instinct was as strong as it was when he sensed an ambush. He'd asked the Pinkerton agent in San Francisco to send out an inquiry about her background, but that might take weeks to learn. In the meantime, Luke was finding it hard—not to mention finding himself in a different kind of hard situation—whenever he thought about her. Which, *unfortunately*, was far too often.

She rarely mentioned Travis, so Luke didn't think she'd established any real affection toward the man, but if she had married him strictly to join with him in swindling, there would be no need to grieve. *Especially* if she were concocting some scheme on her own. Most women didn't decide to run a business by themselves.

Might she even know who the accomplice was?

Luke rubbed his temples, hoping to ward off a headache. Pouring another brandy, he wasn't sure he wanted to find out if she did, but if he orchestrated his own scheme right, he would find out.

****

"We are getting so close to being ready to open the tea room," Abby said to Luke as she surveyed the changes in the storage area several days later.

Luke grinned. "All we need is the tea."

"But that should be here any day, shouldn't it?"

"Yes. It's just a matter of when the ship left the Asian port."

Abby smiled. "I still have a few little things to finish, so it's just as well."

"You've done a good job with the decorating. I would have been at a loss."

She'd almost been at a loss as well, although she wasn't about to admit it. The tiny flat in her mother's tenement had barely allowed room for three narrow cots, a scarred wooden table, two rickety chairs, and a single, small wardrobe that held all of their clothes. The lodgings at the convent after her mother died had been just as sparse.

"I've enjoyed doing it." Thank heavens for Delia. Not only did the woman love to shop, she'd had her own home back in Ohio before she came West. Consequently, the newly converted tea room now boasted a sofa of rich burgundy velvet with a long, low table in front of it that would hold a full tea service plus platters for tiny sandwiches and gooey confectionery sweets. A dozen chairs with dark rose brocaded satin cushiony seats and backs and curved, cabriole legs were scattered about the room with small tables dispersed between them. The walls had been papered a soft gold, while striped burgundy-and-rose curtains hung across the single window in the room, and one wall boasted a painting of a huge floral arrangement, set in a gilded frame. The oak floors had been waxed until they shone. Abby hoped to put an oriental rug in place someday, but for now that could wait.

She felt an inner twinge of excitement as she glanced around. "I'm looking forward to the tearoom's success."

"As am I," Luke replied. "I hope we get a good response once people find out it's open."

"I'm sure we will." She'd sent invitations to the widows Delia had mentioned and almost all of them had expressed an interest in attending an opening day. There were several times she had wanted to tell Luke, but then she kept reminding herself it would be a wonderful surprise for him to see so many ladies show up. "We'll be offering not only a bit of refinement but also a chance for ladies to invest their money independently. It's a rare opportunity."

Before Luke could respond, John cleared his throat behind her. She turned to see him holding a big box.

"This just arrived," he said. "Looks like the silver set you ordered."

"Oh, good!" Abby said as Luke took it from him and

put it on the table. "I was hoping it would get here before the tea did."

"You got your wish then," the shopkeeper replied and went to wait on a customer.

"He seems to be handling the idea of a tearoom rather well," Luke said as she started unpacking the silver.

Abby gave him a wry look. "Probably because it's been keeping me busy and out of his hair. Or maybe I should say 'away from his customers.' "

Luke lifted a brow. "*His* customers? They're the store's customers."

"Well, I suppose they are, but some of the men who come in always ask for him. I guess since he's been here for two years, they've become friends." Abby placed the final pieces of silver on the table. "Once the ladies' club becomes well known, the place will be bustling with new customers."

He studied her, then nodded. "One can hope."

****

One can also hope it fails. John finished rearranging some stock that didn't require rearranging, but kept him close to the doorway where the bitch and Cameron were talking.

The last thing he needed was *new* customers who might overhear snatches of conversation he had with his so-called friends…those who worked as intermediaries for the opium dens. The general store had operated only as a front for more nefarious—albeit profitable— endeavors. Until the bitch arrived.

Why Travis had decided he needed a damn *bride* when the city was teeming with loose women was beyond him. Travis had said something about appearing respectable to lure in more marks, mainly the number of recent widows, due to the mining disaster, who also had money. John supposed the idea of Travis having a wife might help ease those women into confidence…as long as the wife was biddable and didn't have a clue as to her real purpose.

Abigail Clayton was not biddable. She'd had her nose in the accounting books—at least the legitimate ones—and taken way too much interest in how things got done. He'd had a devil of a time keeping her from going into the cellar to bring up stock.

At the moment, there were no barrels of opium down there since he'd had to remove them in the middle of the night, but another shipment was due soon.

If the woman were to discover it, she would have seen her last sunrise.

Chapter Seven

Thank God Delia knew how to serve tea. As Abby looked over the now-crowded storage room turned into a ladies' club, she realized how much social training she was lacking. While the nuns—and her mother—had taught her basic manners, tea was not something that was served. They drank water. A cup of milk was allocated each morning and poured into plain tin mugs, not delicate china cups that had tiny handles not big enough to insert more than one finger into. She was almost afraid to pick one up for fear of it breaking. And the small squares of bread with what looked like a lettuce leaf that Delia called watercress, along with a dab of some kind of paste, had all the crusts cut off. Delia had been ready to throw the crusts out, but Abby insisted on saving them for a bread pudding. Not that she knew how to make a pudding, but she couldn't let food go to waste. There had been too many nights when her stomach had rumbled because it was empty.

Thankfully, since she was in charge of the meeting, she could busy herself with making sure everything ran smoothly and not have to try to manage a cup and saucer or keep the lettuce concoction from sliding off the bread.

Still, apart from her lack of social skills, she was pleased with the turnout. Nearly a dozen women filled the room which had seemed so large when it was empty. From the sound level of the conversations rising, she thought everyone was enjoying themselves. They'd all remarked on what a good idea it was to have a tea room, and several already had made purchases of tea leaves that John was—somewhat less than enthusiastically— putting into small bags for them to take home.

She supposed she shouldn't fault him for scowling when the ladies first arrived. They'd nearly all come at the same time, decorated bonnets on, petticoats rustling beneath their Sunday-best dresses, and chattering like magpies. Even she had felt a bit overwhelmed by the barrage, and she knew by now that John preferred dealing with male customers.

However, there was profit to be made from customers, including these women. From the way the marzipan, ginger cakes, and nutmeg cookies were disappearing off the other tray, Abby was pretty sure the ladies would be purchasing spices as well as tea.

But what she was most anticipating was the look on Luke's face when he saw the number of women at this first meeting. Although according to the ads they'd put out, the official opening of the tea room was tomorrow, Abby had wanted to surprise him. Delia had agreed that inviting the widows to a private "pre-opening" might make them more amenable to considering investing in the products.

She just hoped he'd show up before the food ran out and the ladies decided to go home.

And then, as if she had lured him with her thoughts, Luke filled the doorway. He'd removed his top coat and it dangled from one finger over his shoulder. He must have come prepared to put some last, finishing touches on the room, because he'd rolled up the sleeves of his shirt and it was open at his throat. A ray of sunlight caught his eyes, burnishing them deep gold. With dark hair tousled by the wind and the hint of his shadow of beard outlining his jaw, he looked wild and untamed. Like a panther.

Conversation halted. Some of the ladies held teacups or cookies halfway to their mouths. Interest showed in their eyes, in some more intently than others, and Abby thought she heard several sighs. She frowned. Her mother had told her it wasn't polite to stare. And these women were practically *ogling*.

"What have we here?" he asked, stepping into the room.

This time, she definitely heard sighs when he spoke in that deep drawl of his. Or maybe because he'd moved closer. *Criminy*. A couple of the younger women were practically drooling. Abby was beginning to understand why John had scowled at the lot.

Well, she wasn't going to let that kind of silliness spoil her surprise. She lifted her chin and smiled at Luke.

"I wanted to surprise you. These women are here by special invitation because they are all widows and have independent funds at their disposal." She looked at the ladies. "As I mentioned in the notes I sent around, this is an opportunity for each of you to increase your bank accounts."

Luke eyed the women and then turned his attention to her. "I'm not sure I'm ready to divulge the particulars."

"That's quite all right." Abby beamed at him, proud that she'd taken the time to really study the invoices for the tea, spices, and silks. "I've already thought a lot of this out. Your investors are willing to finance the expansion, but it's the local population..." She gestured to the women. "…who will be using the products and spreading the word to increase sales. As profits increase, we can offer them shares and build an even bigger expansion to the building, strictly for inventory that caters to women." She turned her gaze on the ladies. "You can all become…*entr-…entrepren-… eurs.*" Abby stumbled over the big word, but she loved the sound of it. "Just like me."

Luke cleared his throat. "Yes, but—"

"It would be wonderful working with *you*," one of the youngest widows—Abby thought her name was Rose—said as she smiled coyly at Luke.

"You will help us, won't you?" the other young widow, whom someone had called Mary, asked as she gave him a wide-eyed look.

Abby refrained from retorting that she was the one who owned the store. Instead, she forced a tight smile. "Since Mr. Cameron is a cousin of my late husband's, I'm sure he wants the store to be successful."

"That I do," Luke replied. "I want to be sure that no one who invests in this…store loses her money."

His words brought smiles to even the older widows, and it seemed to Abby that the ladies all sat up a little bit straighter. Both were encouraging signs. "I'm sure we can trust Mr. Cameron to help us."

"Although a few details still need to be worked out," Luke said.

"Of course," Abby answered. "Perhaps by next week's social, we'll have some definite plans. How does that sound?"

A chorus of assenting comments followed her question, and Abby gave Luke a big smile. Her surprise had worked out very well.

****

Thanks to years of playing poker and staring down the barrels of six-shooters, Luke managed to keep his expression impassive as he observed Abigail moving around, talking to each of the women present.

Was she just being friendly or was she working the room like a professional shyster? Her opening spiel to these women about being entrepreneurs had been as smooth a line as he'd heard from any number of snake-oil salesmen...or, in this case, swindlers out to take an unsuspecting victim's money. Widows made easy marks, especially the older ones, and their interest in this venture had not gone unnoticed by him.

He had to wonder again if Abigail had known Travis Sayer before and come West as a business partner.

Not that he hadn't planned to do almost exactly the same thing, albeit for different purposes. He'd meant what he said about no one losing their money, but there was a fine line between setting up a fraudulent investment to draw out Sayer's accomplice and actually committing fraud. He'd be able to handle this scheme much better if a certain blonde didn't tangle herself up in it.

If she was as naïve as she appeared, he had to protect her and keep her out of any kind of involvement. And accomplishing that would take some careful manipulation. He could almost hear her protests already.

His conscience niggled at him. Abigail's protests about staying out of the investing process would be nothing compared to her outrage at having the truth come out about her husband's thefts. She would think him the worst kind of scoundrel for forcing the sale of the store, even if it was to return the lost savings to his grandmother and her friends. She was already seeing it as her livelihood. For the first time since Belle Fontaine had taken him for a fool, Luke realized that he wanted to have a woman's respect. Not just any woman's, though. *Abigail's.*

He gave himself an inward shake to dislodge that thought. Then he sternly reminded himself that *Mrs. Sayer* could very well be the real scoundrel, not him.

She could be…couldn't she?

****

"What do you mean, you will handle the investment dealings?" Abby glowered at Luke across the table at the Occidental Hotel several days later. This time they were having lunch, and this time they were discussing business. So much for Delia's idea of courtship, not that Abby was inclined to feel romantic at the moment, in spite of the elegant surroundings. Luke had practically told her to keep her nose out of operating her own store.

"I'm not going to let anyone take over my store," she announced firmly, and perhaps a bit too loudly as diners at two different tables glanced in her direction. She lowered her voice. "I will not."

Luke gave her an easy grin, the one that made him look devilish and cherubic at the same time. Drat it. She was not going to allow him to charm her out of this. "I want to run my store. I *own* it." Even to her ears, she sounded petulant, but she lifted her chin in defiance anyway.

"I don't remember saying anything about that." He dropped a lump of sugar into his coffee and stirred. "I merely suggested that you let me set up the investment opportunities."

"And I don't remember you *suggesting* anything."

Abby frowned. "You *said* you were going to *take charge*."

"Only of the people who want to opt in to the expansion," Luke answered. "After all, I answer to my investors, and local participation is what they are interested in."

"The expansion will be part of my store," Abby responded, not about to give in. "That will make it part of *my* business."

"That's true. *If* and *when* we actually build onto it."

Luke's tone had been much more amiable than hers. Abby took a deep breath, determined she could be equally as composed. "I thought that was the whole idea."

"It's *part* of it." He took a sip of coffee. "Any group of investors is going to want to make sure the venture will be profitable, so for right now, we'll see how sales go with the spices, tea, and silks."

"That's what we're going to ask the ladies to buy into?"

"For now. Once the widows feel confident they're turning a profit, that will generate more interest from their friends. Then, I'll see how it goes."

"You? What about us?" As soon as the words were out, she wished she could shove them back into her mouth. Good Lord, it sounded like she was asking about them...about him and her...like they were in a real relationship, not just business partners of sorts. Her face warmed. Blast Delia and her romantic notions. "I meant—"

"I know what you meant. You want to be included in anything that has to do with the store."

Abby gave him a wary look. "That's right."

"And I commend you for it." He tilted his head. "Here's a suggestion. For now, while you're still learning how to run your store, let me handle the first part of this investment angle."

"I'm not sure—"

"Let me put it another way, then. If this investment venture doesn't work out, it would be better to have the accounts completely separate from those of the general store." He paused. "It would also be easier, legally, if two different people were in charge…you for the store and me for the ladies' club involvement."

Abby gave him a sideways glance. "You think they'll be more easily persuaded by you to invest because you're an attractive man?"

Luke grinned. "Do you think so?"

She felt herself blush. Her brain seemed fond of making stupid comments today. "Are you fishing for a compliment?"

"Maybe. But I'll go first. I think you're attractive too." He sobered. "Not just beautiful, although you are. But you've got spunk and spirit and determination. I find those qualities highly attractive in a woman."

Abby sputtered, sure from the intense heat radiating from her face that it was probably the color of a sunset. No one had ever recognized those qualities in her before. Oddly enough, they were the traits of which she was most proud. "In that case, I'll admit that I think you're honest and honorable and trustworthy." She managed a small smile and a shrug. "In spite of being thoroughly handsome."

He grinned again. "Am I exceedingly charming, too?"

"Hmmph."

"Come on. Admit that I *might* be persuasive with the ladies' group."

Abby rolled her eyes. "All right. You *might*. So, for now, I'll acquiesce to your wishes. But once we consider building an expansion, I'm on board from then on. Agreed?" She held out her hand to shake.

"Agreed." Luke took her hand and brought it to his lips instead. "Sealed with a kiss."

A riot of sensations shot through her hand and up her arm. The solid warmth of his hand encasing hers, the firm press of his lips, the soft brush of breath across her knuckles… No one in the Bowery made courtly gestures like kissing a lady's hand. And then he turned it over and placed another kiss in her palm, followed by a slow swipe of his tongue. Heat pooled in her belly and her nipples pebbled unexpectedly beneath her bodice. Luke dropped her hand and winked at her as he stood to pull her chair. "I like being thorough."

Flustered, she didn't trust her voice. She just hoped she'd be able to walk, because her knees felt like jelly. There was no denying that Luke Cameron was charming.

And dangerous as a panther.

Chapter Eight

After lunch, Luke walked Abby back to the store, then saddled Diablo and headed past San Francisco's hills toward the relative flatness to the south. The stallion needed a good run and he needed a place that was peaceful and quiet.

Half an hour later, he reined in the sweating horse atop one of the low mesas, slipped out of the saddle, and propped himself against a rock to contemplate.

He felt like a complete ass. Abigail thought him honest and honorable. She'd *said* so. And here he was, devising a plan that might ultimately cause her to lose her store. Regardless of the method of ill-gotten gains that had been used to purchase the place, Sayer was dead. Even though Luke was determined to smoke out the damn accomplice who'd gone to ground, the business, at least for now, was Abigail's. More and more, he sensed she was sincere in wanting to run the general store. She had shown a good aptitude for numbers and understanding accounts. She'd certainly taken a big interest in the new inventory of tea, spices, and silks.

Although he'd gotten no report back from the Pinkerton agency yet, less and less did he feel that she'd had any prior relationship with Sayer. But maybe that was wishful thinking on his part. Which was the other part of his dilemma.

He was beginning to fall in love with her in spite of

his logical mind screaming at him that everything was wrong with that notion. For better or worse—and *those* were definitely the wrong words to use—they were business partners, even if he had ulterior motives. He'd meant what he said about her spirit and independence. She didn't deserve to be used or taken advantage of either in a business situation or a personal one.

He wasn't even sure how capable he was of opening his heart again. Belle had done more than just hurt his pride. She had been the cause of his friend's death by Luke's own hand. All because they had both believed her lies. The tears, the begging for help, the swearing that the bruises had come from the other one along with vows of faithfulness to the one she was hoodwinking had all seemed so sincere. So real. They'd both been fools to believe her, but by then it had been too late. Luke hadn't trusted a woman since then.

What he should do would be to stamp "paid" to the foolish flirtation he'd begun at lunch. He'd only meant to tease her a bit about her remark that she thought he was attractive, in order to sidetrack her dogged determination to be part of the ladies' club plan. That intention had taken wing when she'd blushed so innocently. As far as he knew, women's wiles didn't extend to blushing-at-will. Then, when she'd added he was handsome, he'd reacted like a lad wet behind the ears. Faster than a dust-devil across a Kansas prairie, the stupid question about being charming, too, had escaped his mouth. He'd wanted to see her blush again. Instead, she'd only guffawed, which his smaller head—the one not attached to his shoulders—had taken as a direct challenge. The next thing he found himself doing was kissing and licking her hand, with the word *thorough* stuck in his brain. Fortunately, being in a restaurant quelled his ability to continue to kiss and lick her everywhere. Unfortunately, his nether regions had sprung enthusiastically to life in anticipation of her returning the favor. Even now, just thinking of that possibility—or plunging his wayward shaft deeply into her warm wet sheath—stirred him again. He steeled his thoughts. What he needed to do was plunge into a horse trough of cold water.

He ran a hand through his hair in frustration. Could he trust Abigail? He didn't know. He *wanted* to, but God help him if she'd been in cahoots with Sayer and whoever his blasted accomplice was. He would not have a shred of self-respect left if he allowed another woman to deceive him again. To trust was to be vulnerable.

And yet…a small voice, one he had suppressed since Karl's death, whispered that he should try.

****

Luke Cameron had to be one of the most exasperating men she'd ever met. First—drat him!—he had charmed her into agreeing to let him handle the ladies' club venture. Then, for the past two weeks, he'd mostly been absent from the store and maintained an aloof attitude when he was there. Even John seemed to have noticed a difference in Luke's behavior, for he had taken to watching each of them closely.

Like he was doing now. Abby shuffled through a stack of papers on the desk in the small office, pulled one out, and handed it to John, who stood across from her. "Why was I not told *Neptune's Maiden* would be delivering another shipment of tea and spices this week?"

He shrugged and laid it back down. "I put it in the

stack. I thought you'd see it."

"It was near the bottom." Abby spread the invoices across the desk. "I asked that any imminent deliveries be put on top."

"It must have gotten shuffled. Maybe Cameron looked through the pile."

As scarce as Luke had made his presence known lately, she doubted it. Besides, he'd agreed to let her handle the store's inventory. She hadn't meant that he needed to do some kind of vanishing act. She sighed, knowing it was a bit unreasonable to be put out with Luke because he was letting her have her way. *Staying* out of her way. Not that she'd told him to do that. But then, maybe he was showing her he had confidence in her abilities…

She gave herself a mental shake. Enough with going around in circles trying to figure the man out. If Delia hadn't planted those seeds of romantic interest, Abby wouldn't have taken any notice at all. She grimaced. That wasn't true either. Apart from it being extremely hard *not* to notice a man who stood over six feet tall, and with a commanding presence—especially one with unusual whiskey-colored eyes and a dangerous look—she enjoyed his company. He made her feel…special. She cleared her throat. He probably made every woman feel *special.* She only had to recall the sighs Rose and Mary heaved when he came into the room or the smiles and easy banter he used with all the widows.

"You have something to say?" John asked, his tone surly.

Abby refocused. Dealing with John was an entirely different matter. He was touchy about any criticism regarding his work, insisting on carrying out his duties, from running the cash register to hauling inventory up from the cellar, without assistance. It was almost as though he feared he'd be fired if he let anyone help him. He probably thought her own grumpiness had to do with the ship's invoice not being on the top of the stack. She shook her head and picked up the paper.

"This looks good. We were just about out of spices and had only a few sacks of tea left, so this shipment will be right on time."

John nodded. "I'll make sure everything is put away when it arrives."

She smiled, hoping to sooth ruffled feathers of male pride. "I know you like to work alone, so I'm sure you'll take care of it."

He gave another curt nod and turned away. When he had gone, her thoughts returned to a completely different man. A maddeningly charming and recently elusive man who also liked to work alone.

She sighed again. Luke Cameron was vexing indeed.

****

Two weeks of trying to keep his distance hadn't worked. Luke wasn't sure whether to be angry at himself for letting his iron-like self-will be cracked or amazed that someone who might be a schemer had managed to do so. But, like iron, she seemed to have a magnetic pull on him.

Unfortunately—or fortunately, depending on which of his heads was currently leading his inner battle—Abigail wasn't present when he walked into the store.

"Where is Mrs. Sayer?" he asked John.

The man snorted. "Some of those widow women came by. Something about visiting a dressmaker and needing advice on using silk."

Luke frowned. He'd spent part of his time away from the store talking to the bankers who'd handled the original loans and paperwork on the store—they'd agreed to handle the account for expansion, additionally—but he'd also shown up for the weekly socials at the store. His goal had been to meet new matrons that the ads had drawn in and to drop hints about the investment venture.

Perhaps staying away the rest of the time hadn't been such a good idea, especially if Abigail had started making friends with the ladies. He didn't want her implicated in any way once he'd flushed out the accomplice and the phony set-up was exposed. Her name and reputation should not be jeopardized in any way. His intention was to force the damn man to sell the store quietly without fuss, except for a bit of blackmail, if need be, and hand over the proceeds.

"Is she going to be gone all afternoon?"

"Don't know. She didn't say."

And he didn't ask. Luke sensed the underlying resentment in John's tone. He supposed the man didn't like answering to a woman, but he'd been tempted to remind him that he should be grateful she hadn't given him the sack. Especially now that she had a handle on how to operate the store. But he'd held back, not wanting to make the situation worse. Once the accomplice was revealed, John would more than likely be out of a job anyway.

So would Abigail.

Over the past two weeks, Luke had decided that he'd have to give a portion of the proceeds to Abigail—if she weren't part of the scheme to begin with—so that she'd have enough money for a down payment on another enterprise. She'd definitely shown she had a head for business. Not to mention sales. In less than the month the ladies' club had been open, she'd managed to persuade the ladies to buy almost all of the tea, spices, and silks…which made his mind start circling around in its never-ending cycle of whether she had been part of Sayer's swindling or not. Lucifer's horns! He was going to drive himself straight into perdition if he didn't stop thinking like this. He gave himself a mental shake. At any rate, he aimed to protect her from any fallout that would be his doing.

"If Mrs. Sayer is going to be out, I guess I'll study the profit margin on our new imports," he said. "If they're as good as I think, we may be close to starting to build that extension."

"They're good. I know, since I run the cash register." John cast him a sideways look. "Maybe too good."

Luke raised a brow. "Too good? What do you mean?"

He shrugged. "Just heard her talking. Every time one of them women comes in, she always tells them not to forget that if an extension is built, they could be a part of the business."

That was *not* what Luke wanted to hear. They'd *agreed* to keep the venture separate. How in hell was he going to keep her name out of a possible scandal if she was promoting the damn thing? He sighed. He was definitely going to have to put more time in at the store. "I'll talk to her. I haven't come up with any specific plans yet."

John snorted again. "Maybe you haven't, but she

has."

Luke's gaze sharpened on him. "What do you mean by that?"

"The woman's wily. She ain't one of them docile types."

That was an understatement if he'd ever heard one. But Luke needed to know what John really meant. "I won't argue the point, but I don't understand how it makes a difference."

"She cottons up to all them women. Makes talk real nice." John cast another sideways glance. "She's earnin' their trust."

"Go on."

"I think she's got her own reasons for wantin' you to do this."

"And what would that be?" Luke asked, keeping his tone neutral.

"She spends hours going over them books. Doesn't miss a penny being off."

"That sounds like a good thing to me."

"Maybe." John shrugged again. "Like I said, she's a wily one. Wouldn't be hard for her to doctor them receipts and pocket a bit of money."

Luke wasn't sure he'd heard John actually *say* those words or if his own brain was playing tricks on him from over-thinking. "You think Mrs. Sayer's fleecing her own business?"

"Not sayin' that. A dog don't mess its own bed," John answered, "but I think she's fixin' to double-cross you."

Luke gave him an incredulous stare. "Double-cross me? We're partners."

"Ain't unheard of. She's cagey enough to fix a few

numbers on some of the expenses once the building starts. Maybe even pocket some of the profit from them women she's sidling up to." John lifted one shoulder nonchalantly. "If I was you, I'd keep the locals out of investing in this building thing."

"But my investors want local participation. It's one of their terms." It was Luke's *only* term. He had to spike the interest of whoever the silent partner was. Once word got out that the same bank would be handling the account for the investment, it should catch the attention of the accomplice.

"Just sayin'." John looked over to the door where a customer had entered. "Be right with you." As he turned away, he lowered his voice. "If them local widows get taken in, there's a lot of vigilante justice in this here town."

Vigilante justice. Luke had seen more than his share of vigilante justice. Had administered some of it himself when he worked for Pinkerton. However, he intended to return the widows' money when this was over.

But it was one more reason to keep Abigail out of this mess.

****

John rang up the purchase for the customer who had come in and then stared at the closed door of the office where Cameron had retreated. He had a nose like a bloodhound when it came to smelling a swindle. And one was about to happen.

He just didn't know if the New York bitch or Sayer's "cousin" was setting it up. It could be both. He'd felt like a horse with a cactus thorn under its saddle since they'd showed up. He'd tried to talk Travis out of a mail-order bride, but the damn fool wouldn't listen. Insisted having a "proper" wife would lend him respectability. That she'd never set foot in the store without him. Ha.

Then there was Cameron. Travis had never mentioned a cousin. The man looked more like a professional gambler than a business investor. John had dealt with both, and true gamblers were much more dangerous. They missed nothing. Took nothing for granted. They were definitely not easy to fool.

And John needed to keep up the charade of running a simple general store. It was a perfect cover for the lucrative opium trade that had proved more profitable than any of the swindling schemes he'd been part of. Captain Bartlett had a steady supplier and could deliver monthly shipments. Building an expansion would interfere with the movement of those barrels. His buyers had already complained there were too many people swarming about when they came to the store. Getting a pack of widows involved—the perfect marks for a swindling operation—would mean relentless traffic flowing in and out of the store. He couldn't allow that to happen.

John closed the cash register drawer. He had hoped the bitch would soon tire of playing at running a store, but that hadn't happened. Since she refused to sell and the so-called cousin wasn't going anywhere either, he was going to have to take matters into his own hands.

It was time to make things start to happen. Things that weren't going to be pleasant.

Chapter Nine

"I just knew this club was going to be successful!" Delia handed Abby a plate with a scrumptious-looking puff of pastry on it.

Abby looked around the tea room. Every seat was taken and several ladies were standing, managing to balance tea cups on saucers while nibbling on the new cinnamon-and-sugar sweets that one of the widows had brought. She took a bite of the meringue off the top of the nutmeg-laced biscuit and let it dissolve in her mouth before answering.

"Your idea of having the ladies compete for best desserts was sheer genius."

Delia grinned. "They do buy more spices when they're trying to out-do each other."

Abby smiled back. "Not to mention I don't have to ask the baker to come up with ideas. I'm not very creative when it comes to cooking."

"You won't have to worry about that now." Delia gestured to the guest book lying open on a small table by the door. "Practically everyone who's signed in has indicated dates—that's with an 's' as in plural—that they want to bring their creations. You've got enough volunteers to last three months!"

Abby nodded happily. "Thank goodness the *Neptune Maiden* is due in soon with the next shipment of spices. We're already running low."

"That will just make the widows more competitive." Delia took a sip of tea. "You probably could even raise the prices since they're buying so much."

"Supply and demand, you mean?" Abby shook her head. "First, I don't want to take advantage of them. A lot have become friends over the past weeks. Second, the best way to increase sales is word-of-mouth or, in this case, *taste*-in-mouth. The more they bake and share with other friends, the more will come in here to buy."

Delia reached for a cookie. "I suppose you have a point."

"I also sell spices to the baker, and he's already grumbling about the cost, even though, from his continuing orders, I suspect his customers are appreciating his new additions." Abby wiped crumbs from her fingers with a linen napkin. "I don't want to offer him a discount—at least not yet—while the ladies are paying full price."

"That's really ethical of you."

"I want to be honest, that's all." Abby meant that. If her friend only knew about her past, she wouldn't think her ethical at all. Let alone honest. She and Ben had started their criminal lives by stealing apples from vendors' carts as children and, as adolescents, they'd graduated to snatching unattended purses and parcels, eventually refining their skills to picking pockets. They'd done what they did to survive, but that still didn't make it right. Abby pushed the unwelcome memories away. She was three thousand miles away from her past. No one here need ever know what she had done. Abby smiled at her friend. "Once we start work on the expansion, I can raise prices because the ladies who choose to invest will also be receiving part of the profit."

"And that might encourage the others to do the same?"

Abby nodded. "That will be an option. The more investors, the more we can do. I've done a lot of thinking about how I want to expand and what I want to include. If it works out, everyone will stand to gain."

"And what does your man say about all this?" Delia asked with a twinkle in her eyes.

"Luke is not *my* man." Abby felt her face warm even as she spoke. "He's my business partner, as I've told you before."

Delia shrugged. "Doesn't mean he can't be both."

"You really do have a one-track mind."

Delia grinned, clearly unfazed. "You moped around the boarding house those two weeks he didn't call."

"I did *not* mope!" At least, she hoped she hadn't. Dear Lord! The last thing she needed to be doing was falling in love with Luke Cameron. Abby started. Where in the world had *that* thought come from? Just because he'd been spending more time at the store recently wasn't reason for her to conjure up fantasies. He wasn't one of those knights from King Arthur's court that her mother used to tell her stories of. He certainly wasn't going to pledge devotion to her or anything. "I did not mope."

"All right, if you say so." Delia sounded totally unconvinced. "But I think planning the expansion would be a good way to spend some time with the man." She grinned again. "Just the two of you."

Abby felt her cheeks heat once more. "You *really* are incorrigible."

"I'm also right." Delia helped herself to one of the meringue confections. "So when are you going to talk to him?"

Abby sighed. It was no use trying to persuade Delia otherwise. And perhaps she didn't really want to, if that odd, tingly sensation in her stomach was an indication. "Soon. I'll talk to Luke soon."

****

"You wanted to see me?" Luke asked as he poked his head inside the door to the small office a couple of days later.

Abby looked up from the ledger she was studying. "Yes. Come in. Close the door, please."

"Yes, ma'am." She didn't have to say *please*. Luke bit back a grin as he did as he was told. If the woman wanted to be alone with him in a small space, he wasn't going to complain. The two weeks he'd tried to keep his distance had failed in cooling his ardor. Expecting to get a chill under a hot desert sun would have been a more reasonable outcome. So now he figured maybe he should reverse course. Maybe being in her company—in close company—would do the trick. *Maybe*.

Somehow he doubted the desire that had built up in those two weeks would be sated by sitting across the desk from her. He took the straight-back chair and moved it around to her side, turning it around so he could straddle it. He leaned his arms on the back.

"What would you like?"

Abby blinked. "What would I like?"

He knew he should rephrase the question, but he couldn't help pushing the boundaries a little. Just to see where a bit of flirtation might go.

"What would you like me to do to—for—you?"

The innuendo, stupid as it was, didn't go unnoticed if the pinkish flush to her cheeks was any clue. He had the most absurd urge to grin like an idiot. "You asked to see me."

"Ah. Yes. So I did."

She appeared flustered, and he managed to refrain from a self-satisfied smirk. If he could rattle her with an innocuous comment or two, maybe she harbored a few carnal thoughts herself under that veneer of reserve she wore like her high-necked calico dresses. He'd found women who appeared calm and collected in public were usually the most passionate in bed. Not that he intended to pursue this madness that far. But damn, two weeks' absence and he might as well have been a chunk of iron ore and she a magnet.

"Are we going to spend the rest of the afternoon together?"

Abby blinked again, then shook her head. "This shouldn't take that long."

"Take as long as you like." He gave her an infectious smile, one that usually worked. "I happen to have the rest of the day free."

She frowned instead. Obviously refocusing, she turned the ledger around for him to see. "The profits from the tea and spices have been very good."

"I know that." Luke tilted his head. Abby certainly wasn't acting coy—she hadn't exactly responded the way he'd hoped to the smile, but why the hell would she call him in here to tell him something that was obvious? He knew when the shipments arrived and the quantity as much as Abby did. He glanced at the door again. *She* was the one who'd asked him to close it. Perhaps subtlety wasn't the direction to take. Abby was a direct person. Luke leaned closer over the chair's back.

"Why do you want to be alone with me?"

Her eyes widened, her face turned bright pink, her mouth opened, then snapped shut. Then she practically sputtered, "I wanted to discuss starting the expansion to the store. It's time."

If he had been a balloon and someone had stuck a pin in him, his pride could not have deflated more quickly. While his head—the one on his shoulders—had entertained lustful thoughts and his other head had enthusiastically started to stand at attention, *she* had been thinking about business. Lucifer's horns. Maybe he needed to visit a brothel and take care of his urges.

"I haven't had the chance to do the paperwork yet." He was hoping that, with word getting around, the damn accomplice might start nosing around. "I thought I might give it a few more weeks."

"There's no need to do that." Abby opened a drawer and stuck her hand in to withdraw another ledger. "I've been keeping track of—ouch!"

"*Don't move!*" Lightning-quick reflexes that he'd honed as a gunfighter instinctively came into play. In one fluid movement, Luke rose, pushing the chair down with one hand while the other made a sweeping movement across the desk that sent the ledger flying. An instant later, his boot stomped the scorpion that was trying to scuttle away. He turned to see Abby clutching her hand. Two strides had him by her side.

"Did it get you?"

"I'm…not sure. I started to feel a sting—"

"Let me see." He took her hand, turning it over. He ran his finger over a tiny red dot. "Does this hurt?"

"Only a little." She tried to pull her hand away. "I think you knocked it off before it could do much damage."

He didn't release her hand. "How the hell did a scorpion get inside that drawer?"

"I don't know. I've taken the ledgers out of that drawer lots of times. There's never been even a spider in there." Abby smiled and brushed her other hand along his cheek. "But I owe you much thanks."

Her touch was his undoing. He wrapped his free arm around her waist and drew her closer. Her eyes widened, but she didn't resist. "I can think of a way to say thank you," he said and then lowered his mouth to hers.

****

The moment his lips touched hers, Abby's world started to spin. She suddenly felt off-balance, lightheaded, and like her legs had turned into bread dough. She clutched Luke's shoulders to steady herself and then realized she had drawn herself up and he'd pulled her tight against him. Instead of reflexively pushing away like she always did whenever any man tried to embrace her, she found herself leaning in. His arms around her felt strong and steady, just like the beat of his heart.

Not to mention his mouth. Who knew that a man's lips could be so gentle yet feel so firm? And warm. Well, maybe some women did know, but Abby had never allowed herself to be kissed before. *Really* kissed. And Luke was *really* kissing her.

His lips brushed softly against hers, teasing her into wanting more. Then they pressed more firmly, coaxing her into parting her own. He sucked her lower lip between his teeth and then swept his tongue across the wetness slowly, in a leisurely way, as though savoring fine wine. It tickled and tingled and sent strong sensations vibrating through her body. As he touched the tip of his tongue to hers, playfully battling it, something clenched low in her belly, and when he delved deeper into her mouth to explore it fully, an odd throbbing began between her legs.

A knock on the door to the office brought Abby to her senses as thoroughly as though she'd been doused with a bucket of cold water. Luke released her, but his eyes were dark with desire as he turned away.

"Come in." His voice held a hint of irritation.

She was glad he was the one who spoke, because she wasn't at all certain she was capable of anything but a mere squeak at the moment. Somehow, while they had been kissing, he'd backed her against the desk. She was grateful now for its support since she wasn't at all sure her legs worked.

John stepped inside and looked around. "Everything all right in here?"

Luke frowned. "Why shouldn't it be?"

"I thought I heard a ruckus."

"That was a chair being overturned and the ledger falling." Abby had managed to find her voice. "A scorpion almost bit me."

"A scorpion? Did it get away?" His glance fell to the floor when the insect lay smashed. "Ah, I can see it didn't."

"Hopefully, there aren't any more," Abby said.

"Probably not." John shrugged. "I've never seen one in the store before."

"Still, I'll send someone over to do a thorough cleaning and check on the office," Luke said as he picked up his hat. "I've got to go."

"But we aren't finished," Abby protested, then felt her cheeks heat as she realized how that sounded. Maybe

Luke hadn't caught the unintended innuendo? The thought had no more than popped up when she knew she was wrong. From the way a corner of his mouth—that delectable, delicious mouth that did devilish things to her—quirked up, she knew he had. She swallowed.

"We still have business to conclude."

His eyes darkened to cognac again. "Indeed we do. And I shall look forward to finishing it." He put his Stetson on. "But it will have to wait."

And then he was gone. Abby stared at the empty doorway. He had effectively put the business expansion on hold, but she was pretty sure he wasn't talking about that when he said he looked forward to finishing "it."

She just wondered how long she would have to wait.

****

As he walked quickly toward the stable, Luke knew he had to get away before he concluded what he had started back at the store. Lucifer's horns! What had happened to his iron-will resolve? And, especially, what had happened to his ability to keep his emotions in check? After Belle, he'd sworn he'd never let another female evoke anything more than physical passion from him—fleeting, feel-good-while-it-lasted lust. Pleasure the woman. Satisfy his own needs. Easy and simple.

He doubted anything would be easy and simple—or fleeting—with Abby. His intention had been to give her a simple kiss. Just savor a small taste of her while calming her nerves. Instead, what had started out as slow and easy had erupted into a wildfire quicker than lightning igniting a field of dry hay.

Keeping his distance for two weeks hadn't worked. Obviously, thinking a kiss would quench his feelings was not the right approach either. That had only whet his appetite for much more. Hellfire. The woman was driving him "plumb loco," as the cowboy on the rodeo circuit who'd sold him Diablo had said, only he'd been talking about the horse.

By the time Luke reached the Occidental Hotel, his mind was beginning to function normally again, even if images of Abby's kiss-swollen lips and blue-eyes-turned-violet-with-desire flashed through his brain. He took a deep breath as he entered the lobby. He could control his mind, at least.

"This was left for you." The clerk at the front desk handed him a sealed envelope.

"Thanks." There was no return address, only his name scrawled across the front, but the Pinkerton agency only used proper letterhead when it was sending out invoices for its services. Tucking the letter into his coat pocket, he took out a coin. "For your trouble."

The clerk—a boy who hardly looked old enough to shave—grinned. "The lady who brought it already tipped me. Must be a mighty important letter."

"Could be." He probably thought there was a tryst being arranged. Luke supposed that Isabella, the local agent's daughter, must have delivered the letter since she ran the office, more or less to her father's chagrin. He hadn't really taken notice of whether she was pretty or not. He had a rule about not getting involved with females involved in his work with Pinkerton's, although apparently that rule had taken flight along with his common sense. Still, the kid had a hopeful look on his face and there wasn't any reason to ruin *his* little fantasy, whatever it may be. Luke pushed the coin across the counter. "Let's keep this letter just between you and me."

The boy's grin grew wider and he winked

conspiratorially. "I never saw any letter."

"Good." Luke nodded briskly and walked away, forcing himself to keep his pace slow. Once he was inside his room, though, he tore the envelope open, scanned the contents quickly, then took a deep breath and read it again. Slowly. So the words would sink in.

Forgive the amount of time it took for this investigation, but information on the subject, Miss Abigail Clayton, was difficult to find. However, since Pinkerton's Agency is known for its due diligence— "We never sleep"—*the following are the results of our search.*

1. The last known address for Subject was a convent in the Bowery area of New York City. Apparently, Subject and a brother named Ben lived in a tenement project prior to that.

2. Brother of Subject was arrested for street robbery eighteen months ago.

Female partner eluded arrest, but Subject is suspected to be accomplice.

3. Brother of Subject was released from prison two weeks ago.

4. Subject last seen three months ago and appears to have left the city.

Luke stared at the words, not sure whether to laugh or to roar at being so thoroughly fooled. The little minx certainly was no well-bred gentlewoman like she'd pretended to be…although that did explain her hesitance in using the right flatware at dinner and in serving tea. Not that he cared about any of that. What did stand out, though, was that Abby was suspected of being her brother's partner in street robbery. That certainly explained why she'd been so adept at noticing the street urchin who'd attempted to snatch her purse. She was a pickpocket. Basically, a thief.

Again, Luke wondered if Travis Sayer had known that. Had Abby come to California to distance herself from her past, or to begin a new career in crime by aiding and abetting a scoundrel who was a thief of another sort?

Warring factions rose in his mind. He didn't want to believe that the woman who had kissed him so passionately—the one who had managed to unlock the chains around his heart—was a swindler, but then he'd been deceived before. Falling for Belle's lies had cost his friend his life. He'd do well to remember that. The only feelings he would allow himself would be purely physical. If Abby Clayton was playing him, time would tell.

For now, he'd wait.

At least, Abby hadn't managed to unwrap his heart's chains yet. Mentally, Luke snapped the lock back in place. Then he reached into the tinderbox, struck a match, and lit the letter. Holding it over the cold coals in the brazier, he let it burn until there was nothing left but ash.

Chapter Ten

"Ladies." Luke let his gaze roam slowly over the crowded tea room. "Let me say how pleased I am that so many of you accepted my invitation." The young widows Rose and Mary batted their eyelashes. He briefly smiled at them before acknowledging the rest of the ladies. "I hope you'll find today's information useful."

A week had passed since he'd received the letter from Pinkerton's and decided the best thing he could do for now was his own surveillance…of sorts. That meant, of course, staying close to Abby, which itself created a quagmire of conflicting emotions. At this very moment, he was aware of her presence even though she stood behind him.

To keep from driving himself completely mad, Luke had decided to take action on the expansion. Or, at least, the pretense of expansion. He had to do something toward drawing out the secret accomplice. Generally, ferreting out criminals who had gone to ground wasn't hard. In this case, it might have been easier to find the secret hideout Jesse James used to elude the law.

As he launched into an explanation of costs and how much his "investors" were willing to fund and what portion of local participation "they" were looking for, he also became aware that John was near the door. The man didn't actually enter—having voiced his opinion several times that the women sounded like a gaggle of geese—

but he kept himself busy near the entrance, no doubt to hear what Luke was proposing. Not that Luke blamed him for wanting to know what the plans were, since it affected his livelihood as well.

"So, basically," Luke concluded, "the number of you who are interested in this business venture will determine how much money you'll have to put up front and what percent of the profit from the Far Eastern imports you'll earn each month."

One of the older ladies raised her hand. "My husband invested in stocks once. Does this mean we will own shares of the store?"

"No." Abby spoke in unison with Luke, and he gave her what he hoped was a reassuring smile before he answered the question.

"No," he said again. "Ownership of the physical store will remain the same. You might think of it as Mrs. Sayer 'leasing' us the land to build the expansion, but she will still own it." He saw a few confused looks. "The idea is to use the new room exclusively for the Far Eastern imports, which profits will be exclusively yours. And, of course, to make those profits grow, the ladies' social club will also need to expand." He gestured to the array of competitive goodies on the various small tables. "You might even think about organizing a fair and awarding ribbons."

"I like that idea!" one of the other widows said. "I used to win blue ribbons at the county fair in Kentucky before we moved here."

"And I won blue ribbons in Indiana," another said.

Luke held up a hand before the conversation would turn into a full-fledged bragging competition. "So this discussion has been food for thought. No pun intended."

He picked up his hat to leave. "If today's discussion interests you, please sign the paper on the counter by the door as you leave and also indicate the amount you'd be willing to invest."

He hadn't expected the women to stampede toward the door, but they did, nearly trampling him in their hurry to get to the counter. Guilt niggled at him before he reminded himself that none of these women would lose a single penny. Then anger took its place because they were all so gullible and vulnerable. Sayer and his damn secret partner had taken advantage of people like them.

Spreading the word that the same bank who'd handled the sale of the general store would be handling the expansion hadn't seemed to work. And, maybe, the money had already been laundered and the bank had received what seemed to be legitimate funds. Whoever the silent partner was, he was crafty.

Despite that, Luke had finally set Plan B into action. Now he would start visiting the gambling halls and, feigning drunkenness, let his "scheme" to make a killing of raking in money from unsuspecting women be known.

The accomplice might not be sitting at one of the tables, but a swindler would be willing to take risks—it would be in his blood—and the chances of associating with known gamblers would be high.

There was more than one way to lure a fox from its hole.

Two hours later, after the last of the ladies had gone, leaving nothing but crumbs in their wake, Abby gave Delia a tired smile. "Thanks for helping me clean up."

"It's the least I can do, since I think I managed to sample one of everything."

Abby nodded. "I think I did too. I've got to say, if

all else fails, these ladies could open up a bakery and put everyone else out of business."

"You might not want to mention that to your man," Delia said. "I think—"

"Luke is not *my* man," Abby protested. "I must have told you that a hundred times."

"Probably more," Delia said in that unflappable way of hers. "But 'the lady doth protest too much, methinks.' "

"Doth? Me thinks?" Abby asked as a reason to distract her friend from going down the path of romantic intentions. Again.

"It's from *Hamlet*, the play by Shakespeare."

"I'm afraid I'm not acquainted with the man."

Delia giggled. "I shouldn't think so. He's been dead for three hundred years."

"Oh. Well, I haven't seen the play, either."

"I saw it in New York when my husband took me there once," Delia answered. "Anyway, the line comes when a queen insists she would never marry again if her husband died."

Abby gave her a confused look. "My husband *is* dead. I've not even thought of remarrying. And, for sure, Luke has never mentioned it."

Delia arched a brow. "You're blushing."

"I am not!"

"Are." She waved a dismissive hand. 'We'll see what the future holds."

"For now, the future holds a chance for a business extension," Abby said, thankful for a chance to change the subject. "Maybe we should go see how many ladies signed up."

"I think they all did," Delia said as she followed

Abby back into the general store.

John was studying the list at the counter, but when Abby approached he quickly looked up and shoved it away. Abby smiled. "Do the prospects look good?"

His gaze sharpened on her. "Prospects?"

She pointed to the sheet. "Did most of the women sign up?"

"Looks like a lot of them did," he answered.

As Abby turned the page around to study it, Luke entered from the back entrance. She held up the paper. "You'll like this."

He came over and took it from her. "There must be at least twenty signatures."

"Yes, and it looks like many of them are willing to invest a significant amount."

Abby turned to John. "Don't you think so?"

He shrugged. "I didn't really look at it."

"It looked to me like you were studying it," Delia said.

He narrowed his eyes slightly. "I was just thinkin' about all them women being underfoot all the time."

Abby laughed. "I don't think you need to worry about that. I doubt any of them are going to actually help build the expansion."

"Of course they won't," Luke said as he folded the paper and put it inside his vest. "It's getting late, ladies. I've got a carriage waiting, since Diablo dropped a shoe. May I escort you home?"

"That's not necess—"

"That would be wonderful!" Delia cut in.

Abby refrained from rolling her eyes. Her friend would no doubt try to make something out of Luke's offer.

He smiled at them both and opened the front door. "After you."

Abby walked through the door and started down the short stairs, but as her foot made contact with the second step, the board felt like it slid forward. Her leg buckled and she started to fall, but suddenly strong hands were at her waist, keeping her from landing on the ground.

"Are you all right?" Luke asked.

"Yes." She glanced at the offending board, only to realize it was in place. She felt like an idiot for slipping, although she had to admit she liked the feel of Luke's hands catching her. Supporting her.

And then she realized he still held her. Delia was eyeing her speculatively, probably wondering if she had done it on purpose. Good Lord! What if Luke thought so too? Abby's face flamed. "I'm fine. I just tripped."

"Are you sure?" Luke settled her on her feet, but didn't release his hold. "Try taking a few steps first."

She ignored Delia's grin and took a few steps. "I'm fine. Really."

"The carriage is around the side. Maybe I should carry you."

"I am fine. I was just clumsy." *Criminy*. John was looking out the window. It wouldn't do to have him see Luke pick her up and carry her like she was helpless. She was a business woman. Abby started walking. Fast. Before Luke decided to act like some knight of old.

His laugh tickled her ear as he leaned close, easily keeping up. "I think you've made your point, madam."

"I just don't want you thinking I'm weak."

He sobered. "Rest assured. I would never think you weak."

Behind her, she heard Delia sigh.

Thankfully, the carriage was close, saving her from a reply. During the short ride back to Bartlett's, she made sure to keep the conversation light and casual, even though Delia was giving her pointed looks from where she'd managed to sit across from Abby, forcing Luke to sit beside her. It seemed her friend was bent on playing matchmaker.

As the carriage rolled to a stop, Delia leaned forward to look out her window while the driver hopped down to open the door. "Who in the world is that handsome man standing on the steps?"

Abby looked up as she stepped down and then froze. "Ben! What are you doing here?"

Chapter Eleven

"He's your brother?" Delia looked from Abby to Ben and back as they walked to the porch. Luke did the same, although he remained silent.

Ben gave a little bow. "I am. And to whom do I have the pleasure of speaking?"

"I'm Delia Blake—"

"And I'm Luke Cameron," Luke said. "Your sister's business partner."

"Ah, yes." Ben shifted his gaze to him. "My sister wrote me about you."

Delia tilted her head. "Are you sure you're related?"

"That's what they say, ma'am," Ben replied with an easy shrug.

Delia giggled.

"But you might ask my sister, just to be sure."

Abby nodded when Delia turned to her. It wasn't the first time people didn't believe they were siblings. Ben was as dark as she was fair. Ironically, their difference in coloring had made it easier for them to escape the long arm of the law. Since they didn't look alike, no one had looked for a brother-and-sister pickpocket team.

"We've different fathers," Abby replied. "Ben's was killed in the War Between the States."

"I'm sorry," Delia said, looking back at Ben. "It must have been difficult for you to lose your father at such a young age."

He gave Delia the rakish smile that had so often helped distract their marks on the street. "It was much harder on my mother."

"What a considerate and thoughtful thing to say."

"It's only the truth. A man should always respect the woman who gave him birth."

Delia looked a bit dazzled, a reaction Abby had often seen when her brother decided to be charming. Luke, on the other hand, had narrowed his gaze. "Our mother married Ben's father when she was just fifteen and was widowed at seventeen," Abby said quickly, "and then, two years later, I came along."

"And a better sister no brother could ever ask for," Ben said congenially as he came down the steps to give her a hug. "Abigail has helped me out on many occasions."

She discreetly checked her pockets as he released her, not surprised that the folded wad of money in one of them had disappeared. She raised a brow slightly and received a cheeky grin in return. That had always been his signal that whatever loot they were after had been lifted. They were going to have a *long* talk as soon as they were alone. "Ben does have a knack for getting into trouble."

"Did, Sister, *did*. I'm older and wiser now."

She wanted to question how much wiser, since he'd just demonstrated that he hadn't lost his skill while in jail. Heaven only knew how many things had disappeared in that prison.

"I certainly hope so."

"What brings you out West, Ben?" Luke asked.

"Yes, you never did answer my question," Abby added. "You always said anything west of the

Mississippi was uncivilized."

"That was before you moved out here." He gave her a wistful look, another of his ploys to distract. "You are my only living relation. We should be together."

"How sentimental!" Delia shook a finger at Abby in mock indignation. "You never told me your brother was so devoted to you."

Abby wondered about that. She and Ben had always been close, mostly out of necessity to survive the streets in the Bowery, but after he'd been sentenced and she'd made her decision to be a mail-order bride, she'd made it clear to him that she wanted to start over. She'd never expected him to follow her. Before she could answer, Ben did.

"Why wouldn't I be? We should always appreciate family."

"I agree," Delia said, her expression much like a cat who's just discovered an open door to the creamery. "How admirable."

"And," Ben added, "I did do some research before I started out. San Francisco is booming. It's a city ripe for…entrepreneurs."

Abby gave him a wary look. She certainly hoped he wasn't thinking of teaming up with her to work the streets again. She was finished with that life. Completely finished. If her brother thought differently, he'd be taking the next train back East.

"What kind of a business are you thinking of starting?" Luke asked, his wolf-colored eyes trained on Ben.

Ben had never been stupid, and Abby knew from the slightest twitch of a muscle in his jaw that he'd understood the silent challenge, but his tone was cool.

"I'm going to have to look around, get an idea for what's profitable."

"For now, you could probably help Abby run her general store," Delia said. "Mr. Cameron has investors that want to do an expansion since business is good, and we need all the hands we can get." She smiled. "I help out there as well."

Ben returned her smile. "That would certainly be an incentive."

Delia all but purred. Abby looked from Ben, who blinked at her benignly, to Luke, whose expression had turned predatory. She sighed inwardly. She had a feeling that having Ben and Luke together in the store was going to be more like keeping a schoolyard fight from breaking out rather than amiably working together. For now, though, it didn't seem she had much choice.

But she and her brother were going to have a long, *long* talk first.

****

Luke dismissed the carriage he'd hired, deciding to walk back to the Occidental, hoping to let off the steam building in him like a fully-stoked locomotive ever since he'd met Abby's brother.

Ben reminded him of too many card sharks he'd faced over a number of gambling tables in saloons across the country. Smooth-talking, affable, yet with eyes that missed nothing. Luke had noticed Abby running her hands discreetly over her pockets earlier. He already knew the brother was a pickpocket from the Pinkerton report, but would he actually steal from his sister? If so, then he probably would have no trouble swindling old ladies, either. Was he planning to launch some scheme with his sister? Which only made Luke circle back to his original dilemma about how much knowledge—or involvement—Abby had with Travis Sayer in the first place.

He was going to drive himself completely loco if he kept this up.

Abruptly, Luke changed his direction and headed for the general store. The hour was late and John should be gone by now. It was a good time to examine that step Abby had tripped over. He'd been directly behind her and he could have sworn he saw the board slide as she started to fall.

A few minutes later, Luke approached the store. The light from the street lamp shone into the window, and he detected no movement inside, but for good measure he walked around the building to see if the back was locked. Then he returned to the front and knelt beside the steps.

One side of the step moved easily when he wiggled the ends. The other side remained fastened to the frame, which accounted for why the board didn't completely slide off. He pushed it back into place, then used the palm of his hand to push it forward much like a foot would. The board slid out again. He repeated the movement several times and, without fail, the board slipped each time.

Luke frowned. He had used the back entrance today, but as loose as the step was, why hadn't any of the other ladies tripped earlier this afternoon? Nearly two dozen of them had arrived and departed using the front entrance.

He ran his fingers along the board, noting the fresh wisps of wood threads protruding from the holes. His hand swept the ground, searching for the nails, but he found nothing. That was odd, if the board had come loose after the ladies had departed. Nails didn't just disappear if they'd been torn out by accident.

The sixth sense that alerted him to danger flared like dried kindling struck by lightning. Something was wrong.

And then he got the feeling he was being watched. Without moving his head, he scanned the streets for any type of movement and detected nothing. He attuned his hearing, but he only heard the normal sounds of a horse clopping on cobblestones and the distant barking of a dog. Still, the feeling persisted, and Luke had learned long ago to trust his instincts.

Slowly, he rose and moved away from the light and into the shadows. His mind was on high alert, his body ready for action as he waited.

And nothing happened. After a good half hour of staring down an empty street and keeping an eye on anything that moved in the dusk, he finally turned and left, but the feeling of danger stayed with him.

Something was wrong.

****

Was the bastard never going to leave? John had not moved from behind the counter since he'd first heard footsteps approaching. He'd been about to go but thought perhaps one of his opium buyers needed to see him. They'd started coming around after hours since there were too many nosy women milling about the place since that damn tearoom opened.

He'd nearly been to the window when he caught sight of Cameron and scuttled quickly out of view. He'd doused the oil lamp already, so the store was dark, but he supposed he could come up with an excuse for his late presence if Cameron actually came in.

But the man hadn't. Instead, he'd remained by the

door, scraping and scratching around the steps. That could only mean one thing.

The bastard suspected the board had been loosened on purpose. It had been stupid of John to take the nails, but after the damn gaggle of geese finally left, he'd had to hurry to get the board loose before the New York bitch finished cleaning up.

He didn't like having to hurry. He preferred to be methodical, to double-check, and to always cover his tracks. He was proud of his ability to think things through logically. Laundering money was his special talent. He and Sayer had been about to embark on another scheme—until the idiot had gotten himself killed.

The plan Cameron was proposing wasn't a bad one. Getting the widows to invest and then having the expansion scheme somehow collapse—most likely the "investors" would bow out, after the women's portion had already been supposedly spent on blueprints, permits, and supplies—could work.

As lucrative as the opium trade was, it never hurt to diversify. The list he'd studied earlier told him there was a rather tidy sum just waiting to be laundered, and he'd be the man to do it. First, though, he had to find out how legitimate Cameron's "investors" really were…if they existed at all. The general store was a great cover, or at least it had been before that mail-order bride showed up. He could have handled her if she hadn't insisted on learning to run the business.

She hadn't been bitten by the scorpion he'd put in the drawer. She hadn't fallen off the step that he'd loosened. John narrowed his eyes thoughtfully and then he smiled.

There were lots of accidents just waiting to happen.

Chapter Twelve

Abby looked at her brother from across the table at a small tavern down the street. Even though the food was much better in the public room at the boarding house, the problem was that it was…public. Delia would have wanted to sit with them, and Mrs. Bartlett, after checking Ben into a room on another floor, hovered. Even though she pretended not to be curious, her ears had obviously perked up when they'd been in the lobby.

"So why did you really come all the way out here?" Abby asked.

Ben popped a bite of steak into his mouth, chewed, swallowed, and then shrugged. "There wasn't much reason for me to stick around the Bowery."

"New York City is a big place. You could have found work."

He grinned. "I'd need a partner to return to work."

Abby glanced around, hoping no one was listening to their conversation. She didn't recognize anyone, and the noise level from other conversations was loud enough that they shouldn't be heard. Nevertheless, she leaned forward and dropped her voice. "I am finished with that kind of *work*."

Ben gave her a skeptical look. "As crowded as San Francisco is, the place is wide open for…" He too glanced around. "…our particular skills."

"*No.*"

"No?" He raised a brow. "Why not?"

"Because I have an opportunity to become an honest, bona fide businesswoman."

"That wasn't what you told me when you visited me in prison before you left." He jabbed another piece of meat. "You said Sayer was rich and you were going to take full advantage of his bank account."

Abby flinched. She had said that. In retrospect, it sounded harsh. But then, Travis had been a stranger. It wasn't like she'd come West because she was in love. "I meant that I wouldn't have to worry about money."

"For you and me, growing up like we did, there'll never be enough money."

She knew what Ben meant. His father had been on the wrong side of the war, so there'd not been any compensation from the Army. Her own louse of a father had flitted off without a thought of support. Their mother's meager wages as a laundress barely paid for a single room in the tenement. She remembered distinctly the day she'd overheard their landlord offering to reduce the rent in lieu of personal "favors" from her mother. Abby hadn't known what that meant at the time, but Ben did. It was shortly afterwards that they'd started their "career" as pickpockets.

"I understand, but the store is actually doing very well."

He studied her. "Well enough to risk whatever profit you're making by expanding?"

"I'm not really risking anything. Mr. Cameron has a group of investors—"

"Have you met them?"

"Not personally. They're from the East."

"Are you sure?"

Abby frowned. "What do you mean?"

"What do you actually know about running a business?" Ben took a swallow of tea, grimaced, and set the glass down. "That guy could be a confidence man."

"Luke?" Abby shook her head. "I mean, Mr. Cameron?"

Ben gave her a sharp look. "You're on first-name terms? Has he tried to take advantage of you?"

"Don't be silly." She tried not to think about their kiss and hoped she wasn't blushing. "We're business partners."

"How did that happen, exactly?" Ben asked.

"Mr. Cameron is Travis's cousin, or was," Abby replied. "He showed up shortly after I arrived and told me Travis had decided to expand the store since it was doing so well."

"That sounds like a scam."

"It's not a scam," Abby said sharply. "He had papers."

Ben leaned back and folded his arms across his chest. "They're easy enough to forge."

"The bank accepted them." Abby glared at her brother. "Why must you always be so suspicious?"

"You're asking me that, when we both grew up on the streets?" A muscle clenched in his jaw. "Being suspicious is what's saved my hide more than once."

Abby relented. There had been too many narrow escapes to count, and when she was younger, Ben had protected her often. "I really don't think there's any kind of scam going on, but if you want to take Delia's offer to help out in the store, you can see for yourself."

A corner of his mouth lifted. "Well, she is a 'right pretty little filly' as the cowboys out here say."

"Delia is my *friend*. Don't pull any of your shenanigans with her."

He gave her a wide-eyed look that was a little too innocent. "I don't do *shenanigans*."

Abby wasn't about to be fooled. "Whatever you want to call it then. She's off-limits to you."

Her brother arched a brow. "Like *Luke* is off-limits to you?"

"Luke—*Mr. Cameron*—has nothing to do with this conversation. I've watched you flirt before. I don't want to see Delia hurt."

Ben held up a hand. "I don't want to hurt her."

"See that you don't then." Abby leaned forward and lowered her voice again. "And keep your skilled fingers off the till, as well. No shoplifting."

"I wouldn't even think of it."

"No? You took that wad of money out of my pocket earlier without any trouble."

Ben grinned and reached into his vest to bring out Abby's money. He handed it back to her. "Just wanted you to know I haven't lost my touch."

She snatched the bills up. "Consider yourself retired."

He sighed. "All right, sister dear, I will…at least, for now."

****

"Just put it right there." Delia pointed to a spot next to the pickle barrel for the trunk-sized wooden box that held pounds of beef jerky.

"All right," Ben said as he set the heavy item down. "There are a few more things out in the delivery wagon that I'll bring in."

Delia beamed at him. "You've been such a help this

past week."

He tipped the new cowboy hat he'd decided to start wearing. "I aim to please, ma'am."

"Please call me Delia."

Ben glanced across the room to where Abby stood watching. "I don't rightly know if that's allowed in these here parts."

Delia giggled and Abby rolled her eyes. If her brother put any more twang in his speech, no one would be able to understand him. For some unfathomable reason, in the nearly ten days he'd been in San Francisco, he'd decided to play cowpoke. Not that he'd have a clue what to do should a real cow cross his path. She doubted whether he'd even be able to stay astride a horse at any more than a slow walk. Neither of them had ever taken riding lessons. That didn't stop him from attaching spurs that jangled when he walked in his shiny new boots.

Abby suspected he was playing a part, much like he'd done when they worked the streets and he'd decide which roles they'd act out while fleecing a victim. When they were little, he'd make her pretend to be ill and he'd ask some nice person to help his poor sister. As they'd matured, he'd developed a toothy grin and a cheeky street-urchin way of talking to distract the mark. By the time they'd reached adulthood, he'd learned to flirt and compliment the ladies, often wearing dapper clothing that had been heisted from a rack while Abby kept the shopkeeper's attention with lots of questions about various weaves and weights of coats and such. Since she'd refused to act coy and flirtatious herself, she'd actually learned something about clothing. She eyed Ben's outfit, hoping he'd paid for it.

Delia giggled again and Abby sighed. Even though

she'd warned—threatened—her brother not to lead Delia on, there wasn't much she could do about stopping her friend from sticking close to him whenever she could. Abby had hinted her brother tended to break hearts, but Delia had scoffed at that, saying she liked the attention.

"I thought your brother wanted to pull his weight around here," Luke said as he came to stand beside her.

In spite of her own thinking that there was way too much dallying going on, Abby bristled. "He's unloading the delivery wagon."

"So far, he's brought in one thing."

Before she could answer, John staggered through the doorway, carrying several sacks of flour. Abby had a sudden vision of the man tripping, ripping open a sack, and having half the store look like a white Christmas. She hurried toward him, but Luke got ahead of her, deftly hoisting a couple of the bags to the safety of a shelf.

"I could use a little help out there," John glared at Ben. "I thought you were coming back out."

"I am," Ben replied lackadaisically, "in a minute."

"How about right now?" Luke asked and walked past him. "We can both help."

Ben grimaced and then tipped his hat to Delia again. "Excuse me, ma'am. It appears I'm direly needed elsewhere."

"You just go on then," Delia answered with a grin and a tone Abby had never heard her use before. "We can finish up later."

"Finish up?" Abby asked when the men had all gone outside. "What were you doing besides talking?"

"Ben was asking all kinds of questions about San Francisco."

Abby felt herself go on high alert. "What kinds of

questions?"

Delia blinked at her sharp tone, and she winced. "I'm just wondering, since my brother can be a little nosy sometimes."

"I don't think he's nosy at all. Curious, maybe, but that's a sign of intelligence."

Abby couldn't deny Ben was smart, but usually when he went into questioning mode it was because he'd come up with another way to separate people from their wallets and he wanted to cover all the pitfalls before attempting a new operation. "What was he wanting to know? Maybe I can help."

"He was asking where were some nice places to take a lady." Delia smiled. "I think he intends to invite me to go with him to one of them."

That might be true, but knowing her brother, Abby suspected wanting to know where "nice places" were was simply a ploy to find out where rich people went. People who carried a lot of money.

But Ben was still her brother and she couldn't come out and say he'd had a career as a pickpocket. He *said* he'd mended his ways. She wanted to believe him. She certainly didn't need to besmirch him. Luke was already testy around him, and John sent him sullen looks and wouldn't let him anywhere near the till. Not that *that* was a bad thing. It was one less problem for Abby to worry about. Ben deserved a chance to redeem himself, just as she had. She just hoped her brother wasn't playing Delia false.

****

Abby looked up from the desk as the door to the office opened and Luke stepped inside. As always, his presence seemed to fill the small room, maybe more so today because Ben was already there. The tension between the two of them was nearly palatable. Luke was still suspicious about why Ben had come to San Francisco, and her brother didn't think Luke was who he claimed he was. They reminded her of two lobo wolves circling each other. New terminology for her. Maybe she was acclimating to the West after all.

She shoved aside the ledgers she'd been showing to Ben. He'd asked her to trust him to run the till—under John's supervision—and said he wanted to learn about running a business. She'd been explaining various procedures. Luke had given her a questioning look when she first mentioned she was going to let her brother look over the accounts, but she had to give Ben a chance. At least Luke didn't know about their previous "careers."

"Did you need something?"

"I was going to talk to you about the expansion." He glanced at Ben. "I can come back."

"Don't let me stop you." Ben leaned back in his chair, causing the front legs to lift slightly, and crossed his arms. "I want to hear more about it since it will be part of the store."

Luke frowned. "Nothing you need to be concerned about, since it's being funded independently and no risk to the store's profit margin."

Ben glared back. "Then why bother my sister?"

Abby decided to interrupt before the two of them started sparring for real. She could practically hear both growling. "Luke's not bothering me, Ben. I want to know about all aspects of what's going on, even if I'm not directly involved."

"That's the problem," Luke said.

She felt her eyes widen in surprise. "You want me

directly involved?"

"No, I do not."

"Then…" Abby furrowed her brows in confusion. "What is the problem?"

Luke took a deep breath. "We agreed you'd not interfere—"

"I haven't!"

"You have. You've been talking to the ladies about ordering more and different inventory for the expansion once it's done."

Abby's chin jutted out. "I am just being helpful."

"Do you have a problem with that?" Ben asked.

Luke gave him a cool glance and turned his attention back to Abby. "The plan was—and *is*—for the expansion investment to be kept totally separate from the operations of the general store. That way, if anything goes wrong—"

"What could go wrong?" Ben's gaze sharpened on Luke. "There's nothing shady going on, is there?"

"Ben!" Abby couldn't believe he'd said that. "There's no reason—"

"It is all right," Luke said, his tone measured. "A brother should be protective of his sister."

Ben gave him a level look. "And I am."

Luke stared back. "So am I."

Criminy. If the office were any bigger, they'd be squared off like two gunfighters facing each other on the street. Abby gave each of them a smile which neither returned. She sighed inwardly. "Thank you both for being so protective, but I don't see what that has to do with the expansion."

"We've discussed this before. If anything were to go wrong…" Luke paused and gave Ben another penetrating stare. "…anything at all, and the expansion fell through, I don't want there to be any financial obligations on the part of the general store." Luke turned to Abby. "If you keep talking to the ladies like you're a partner, it could have ramifications. I'm just trying to ensure nothing happens to your store."

Ben gave him a wary look. "That makes sense, I suppose."

"Of course it does." Luke shook his head. "But sometimes your sister can be a bit stubborn."

Ben grinned suddenly. "*Sometimes* is an understatement. I could tell you stories—"

"That's quite all right," Abby said quickly. "And I am *not* stubborn."

A corner of Luke's mouth quirked up. "Maybe I should hear those stories."

Ben nodded. "Glad to tell them."

She glared at both of them. Now they were going to be co-conspirators? "I don't think—"

"Sorry to interrupt." John stood in the doorway. "But there's a gent out here who claims he was shortchanged an hour ago when he bought tobacco." He looked at Ben. "You waited on him."

Ben glanced past him to the customer waiting across the room. "I did. He bought the tobacco, then asked for change on a double eagle. After that, he wanted to switch out some silver for a gold eagle, and then he bought some ammunition." Ben shrugged. "I didn't shortchange him."

"He says you did."

"How much does he claim?" Luke asked.

"Ten dollars," John replied.

"Tell the man he'll have to wait until we count the till this afternoon," Abby said. "If we're over, we'll return his money."

John paused as if he wanted to say more, then gave a curt nod and turned away. After he left, Abby turned to her brother.

"I didn't do it," he said.

She wanted to believe her brother, but she knew how easy it was to confuse a customer with change-outs.

It didn't help that Luke was also giving him a contemplative look.

"I didn't do it," Ben said, standing up so suddenly he knocked his chair down. "I didn't do it."

Then he stomped out the door, leaving Abby and Luke in an awkward silence.

Chapter Thirteen

The till was short not only by ten dollars but by twenty. The double eagle was missing.

Luke watched Abby put the tray back in the register. He could see the disappointment in her eyes. A part of him wanted to draw her into his arms and offer comfort, but with John standing there, he stayed where he was.

He should be keeping his emotional distance also. He'd reminded himself just last night why he had come to San Francisco. His grandmother and her friends were swindled out of thousands of dollars and he was here to make sure they got it back, even if it meant forcing the sale of the general store. The accomplice who laundered Sayer's money still had not surfaced. He needed to be concentrating on luring the bastard out, not empathizing with Abby about whether her brother was still a criminal.

Still, he wanted to wipe the look of desolation from her face. "Since the till is not over, the complaint from the customer that he was shortchanged is moot."

"There's a double eagle missing," John said before Abby could respond.

Luke resisted the urge to plant his fist in the man's face. "It could have been used as change for another purchase."

"A twenty-dollar gold piece? We didn't have no customers come in that needed that kind of change." John snorted. "Ben admitted himself he took the piece in."

"Maybe—"

"He's right," Abby said. "Ben did say the customer had a double eagle. It should be here."

"That doesn't mean Ben took it."

John narrowed his eyes. "Are you accusing *me* of stealin' it?"

"I'm not accusing anyone. I'm saying maybe we should wait until Ben gets back and ask him about it." Hell, he didn't know why he was defending the man. He'd been suspicious of Abby's brother from the start, knowing what he did about Ben's past. He'd almost voiced his disapproval of her brother learning the business, but she'd been determined to give him a fresh start—not that anyone was supposed to know that—and Luke hadn't wanted to squash her aspirations. Even now, the look of hope that flashed across her face caused warmth to course through him.

"That's a good idea," she said. "Ben wouldn't be so stupid as to take something that would obviously be spotted missing. We don't often get that kind of money."

"I'm sure there will be a rational explanation," Luke replied, although he didn't know what it could be. He wasn't one for gratuitous statements, but her thankful little smile tempted him to throw caution to the winds and embellish even more.

"So you're saying he would take something that might not be missed?" John asked.

Luke managed to refrain from bringing his suddenly clenched fist across the man's jaw. Abby's expression fell like a pile of wood that had been stacked improperly. He saw desperation in her eyes and realized she was thinking her brother probably would do just that, in spite

119

of an opportunity to stick to the straight and narrow. Once again, Luke wanted to plant his fist where it would make a satisfying, resounding crack when it loosened a few of John's teeth.

"My brother has no reason to take anything from the store," Abby said, but her voice trembled.

"There's nothing more to be done at the moment." Luke turned to the shopkeeper. "I suggest you go ahead and close up while I take Mrs. Sayer home, since it's getting late."

For once, she didn't argue that she was perfectly capable of seeing herself home. Instead, she walked to the peg that held her coat, folded it over her arm, and then turned. "I'm ready."

Luke knew she meant only that she was ready to go, but a lower extremity stirred to life at her words. He gave himself a mental shake. He'd already let his emotions control his feelings toward the woman who would be the innocent victim if he had to force the sale of the store to recoup his grandmother's losses. And now his body was reacting to innocuous words like a randy lad. Which immediately created another image of Abby, waiting for him. It was a good thing he had Diablo hitched to the cabriolet outside. Driving would keep his hands from wandering.

Abby was giving him a curious look and he wondered if his feelings were showing. Damnation. He always controlled his expressions. Gunslingers had to. If Abby somehow could decipher his thoughts, he was in more trouble than he thought. Hellfire! Luke clenched his jaw as he clamped his Stetson down almost to his ears.

"Let's go." He wasn't about to say he was "ready"

too.

John watched them leave and then smiled as he fingered the double eagle in his pocket.

Abby wondered at Luke's silence as they walked around the side of the building to where the carriage was waiting. Did he think her brother had taken the twenty-dollar gold piece? She wanted to defend Ben, to say he would never pilfer something from his own sister—she *knew* he wouldn't—but that would just sound like there was a possibility he might do such a thing elsewhere. And *that* was something she wasn't altogether sure he wouldn't do. She hated doubting her brother.

Diablo stamped a hoof impatiently as they came around the corner. Then he whinnied shrilly.

"Whoa, there," Luke said, rubbing a hand down the stallion's neck. "I didn't make you wait all that long."

The horse tossed his head and tried to rear, but the hitching post rope was still attached to his harness.

"Easy there," Luke said softly.

Diablo snorted his disapproval and pawed the ground again.

Luke frowned. "Did something spook you?"

Abby looked past them into the small, cleared area. "I don't see anything blowing around."

"Paper or trash wouldn't rile him." Luke unsnapped the tether. "Most likely he needs a good run."

Kind of like Ben did, Abby thought. She remembered when they were kids, and the way Ben would work off his frustration by running. It was a skill that also came in handy when he had to get away from a mark fast. As upset as he was when he left, he might very well be running along the wharf right now. She worried her lip. In San Francisco, especially the Barbary Coast area, the sight of a running man usually meant he'd committed a crime. With corruption running high, there were any number of vigilantes who took it upon themselves to enforce the law before a constable could arrive.

"Do you suppose we could drive by the docks on the way home?"

He looked at her. "It's getting dark. An open, two-wheeled buggy isn't exactly the safest thing to be driving."

"My brother might have gone down there."

A brow lifted. "Why would he do that?"

After she explained, Luke nodded. "Let me take you home, and then I'll saddle Diablo and go take a look around."

Abby shook her head. "That might be too late. I've been here long enough to know a lot of men shoot first and ask questions later."

Luke hesitated, as if having a private argument with himself. "All right," he finally said. "Just keep your hood over your head. No need to go looking for more trouble."

"More trouble?"

"There are some things about San Francisco's Barbary Coast that are the same as the one it's named after."

"Such as?"

Luke paused. "The ships that come in from the Orient sometimes take human cargo back with them."

"*Human* cargo?"

"Yes." A muscle twitched in his jaw. "Female cargo. Women that will be sent to the Middle East and forced to join harems."

Abby felt her eyes widen. "Surely you jest!"

"No. I'm dead serious." He looked at her hair. "They especially like blondes."

She felt herself shiver. "You're just trying to scare me."

"Is it working?"

It was, but she wasn't about to admit it. "No."

He sighed. "Then think about this. Some sailor who's spent too much time at sea might get ideas."

Abby frowned. "But I'm not a...a...one of *those* ladies."

"Being down there at this time of night might make a man think differently."

"But I'll be safe since I'm with you."

His eyes darkened and he muttered something she couldn't hear clearly. "You've got your gun. You can always wave that around to scare anyone off."

He grimaced. "No one in his right mind waves a gun around."

She felt somewhat chastened. "You know what I mean. Out here, a six-shooter can be the law." Luke stared at her for a full moment without speaking and she began to fidget. "I mean—"

"I know what you mean," he nearly growled. "Just get in the buggy."

She climbed onto the bench and slid over, giving him room to sit, and tucked in her skirts.

"The hood," he said.

"I'll put it up when we get close to the water."

"Now."

Abby's chin jutted out.

"Now. Or I take you home."

She grudgingly complied, wondering what made him so annoyed. He was probably put out that he was having to look for her brother. They certainly weren't friends, but she'd hoped the bit of camaraderie they shared at her expense—she was not *that* stubborn— might have ignited a bit of tolerance. Abby glanced sideways at Luke, but seeing the tight set of his jaw, she decided it best to remain silent. At least for now.

They went down Montgomery and then onto Pacific Street, past the dance halls and saloons. Abby stared wide-eyed at the scantily clad women on the sidewalk, some of them waving coyly at Luke. She turned to him and her hood fell back. "Do you know those—"

"*No*." He glanced at her before letting his gaze sweep the area. "Keep the damn hood up."

"You don't have to curse."

"Then don't make me."

Abby glared at him as they turned on East Street and neared the docks. He certainly had become surly. Was it too much to ask… "Oh!" She clapped a hand over her mouth as two men suddenly stepped out from an alley.

"Looks like we struck it lucky twice," one of them said as he brandished a knife.

"Yeah. Good horseflesh and a real nice-looking filly too," the other one answered and flicked his own knife open.

"You can give them up real easy and live," the first one said to Luke as he reached for Diablo's bridle.

Then everything became a blur. Diablo reared, striking out with his front hooves as Luke dropped the reins and rose in one smooth motion. Abby never saw him draw his gun, but the burst of noise and the smell of gunpowder reeled her senses. Seconds later, the men ran off, each of them clutching a bleeding hand.

The commotion had created a stir. A number of

unsavory sorts, as well as some sailors, started swarming toward them.

"Hold on," Luke said grimly as he gathered the reins. "We're going home."

Abby didn't need to be told twice and neither did Diablo. While she clutched the side of the narrow seat tightly, the horse careened down the uneven cobblestones and then onto a rutted road that led away from the wharf. It didn't take long before the sounds of the mob behind them faded away. As Luke slowed the stallion, Abby turned to him. "What..." she started to say, and then her words were lost as a loud crack rendered the air like thunder.

The carriage lurched sideways and she felt herself hurtling through the air.

Chapter Fourteen

The thunder continued to roll over her, a constant rumble accentuated with loud, booming blasts. As Abby slowly regained consciousness, she became aware the noise was angry male voices.

She slit an eye slightly. Ben stood on one side of the bed that she lay in, Luke on the other. They were glaring at each other.

"You must be crazier than a loon. What were you thinking, taking my sister down to the docks at night?" Ben demanded.

"She was looking for you, hothead."

Abby opened her eyes before one of them decided to throw a punch. Everything already hurt. She didn't want to be caught in the middle of—or under—flailing fists.

"What happened?" Her voice came out in a croak.

"You're awake!" Luke and Ben spoke in unison as though they'd practiced it.

She started to smile, but her face hurt. Tentatively, she reached up to touch her cheeks, only to have her hands grabbed, one on each side.

"Careful," Luke said. "Your face got scraped when you landed in the dirt."

"All because of *you*," Ben said.

"*You* were the one who ran off."

"Stop!" Her voice was still weak, croaking, "What

happened? I remember riding in the buggy, and then there was a loud crack—"

"The wheel came off. I think the axle broke," Luke replied.

Ben scowled. "You should have known your fancy little carriage wasn't built for roads like those."

Luke gave him a cool stare. "I wasn't planning to be in that area, remember?"

"Enough, you two!" Abby struggled to sit up. Immediately, Luke bent to assist her. At least, he tried to, until Ben shoved at his hands.

"I'll do it," Ben said.

"I've already got her," Luke answered.

They glared at each other, each holding one of her arms.

"Could you both let go?" Abby asked. They both started, and for a moment she was afraid she was going to be the center of a tug-of-war. Blessedly, they both came to their senses. In another minute, she was propped against the headboard, a stack of pillows plumped behind her.

"Now," she said before they could start arguing again. "Ben, I asked Luke to take me to the docks because I thought you might have gone down there."

"Why would I do that?"

"I know you like to run when you're angry, and the docks are the flattest place in San Francisco," Abby answered, "but it's dangerous, too."

Ben tilted his head toward Luke. "Too bad *he* didn't think of that."

"He did," Abby replied before Luke could. "I had to argue with him about it. He wanted to take me home and *then* go looking for you."

Ben glanced at Luke. "Why would you come looking for me?"

"Because your sister was concerned that you'd get beaten up."

He frowned. "I can take care of myself."

Luke shrugged. "Tell that to your sister, not me."

Ben gave her a determined look. "He should have told you no and stuck to his guns."

"That works?" Luke asked.

"Not usually," Ben admitted. "But, damnation, you put my sister in danger—"

"Not really," Abby interrupted. "You should see how fast Luke is with a gun."

When two pairs of male eyes turned on her, she realized her error. "What I mean is—"

"What happened?" Ben asked, his tone as dark as his gaze.

"Actually, everything turned out all right."

"I don't think so, given your condition." He turned to Luke. "*What happened?*"

Luke glanced at her before he spoke. "We got jumped by a couple of hombres who wanted my horse." He lifted a shoulder nonchalantly. "I wounded them."

Abby breathed a sigh of relief. He wasn't going to tell her brother that the men had also wanted her. "You should have seen him, Ben. He moved so fast, I didn't even know his gun was out until I heard the shots."

"Really?" Ben scrutinized him. "You must have had a lot of practice."

"Some," Luke answered. "Knowing how to shoot straight comes in handy in these parts."

"And he did," Abby said. "He shot their hands and made them drop their weapons."

Ben lifted a brow. "Weapons? They had *guns*?"

"Knives." Luke shrugged again. "Shooting seemed the best way to stop them. I didn't want my horse to get slashed."

Abby was going to make sure Diablo got a nice, juicy apple for his role. Ben would be furious if he found out the rest. "So Luke thought it best to get his horse out of harm's way."

"At breakneck speed?" Ben still looked upset, but his voice had calmed.

"The shots attracted a crowd. I thought it best to get your sister out of there before someone saw or recognized her. It'd be bad business for the store."

She felt her eyes widen and then glanced down before Ben could see her surprise. She hadn't even thought of those consequences, but how clever of Luke to bring that up instead of the fact that she had been in danger herself.

"I suppose you're right about that," Ben said grudgingly. "I suppose I should thank you."

"No thanks needed," Luke said. "I'm glad I was there."

Ben gave him a long, silent look, then slowly nodded.

Luke's words sent a warm tingle through her in spite of everything hurting. He definitely deserved a reward for both his quick action and his quick thinking in response to her brother's questions, but she doubted he'd be interested in an apple. Perhaps another kiss? When her brother wasn't around. Heat pooled low in her belly, making her forget the aches and pains for a moment. She'd look forward to awarding that kiss.

****

Early the next morning, Luke got a wagon from the stable and returned to the spot where the cabriolet had broken down. The small carriage was still where he'd left it, on its side and pushed to the edge of the road. After the accident, he'd unhitched Diablo and ridden bareback to the boarding house. Thankfully, the horse was so attuned to him that he only had to guide him with his thighs, leaving his arms free to hold an unconscious Abby.

He didn't think he'd ever forget the sight of her flying through the air or the sound of the hard *thud* when she hit the ground. From the way her face was scraped, it appeared she'd landed on her side and skidded a few inches. He'd never forget, either, how his heart had pounded so hard he was afraid it might escape his chest when he'd knelt beside her still body. He'd prayed—something he hadn't done in a long time—that she still breathed, and tears had actually streamed down his face when he felt her heartbeat. He couldn't remember crying since he was a small child. Last night, though, that had not mattered. It was only after the physician had come, done his examination, and said she had a mild concussion but would live, that Luke realized a truth.

He loved Abigail Clayton Sayer.

Luke picked up the wheel that had come off and started to toss it inside the wagon bed. Then he stopped and looked more closely. The wheel wasn't broken. Luke grimaced. The bolts holding it onto the axle must have loosened because of the rutted road and the speed at which he drove. His stupidity might have gotten Abby killed. He could have slowed Diablo once they were clear of the crowd that had gathered. Or he could have taken a different street, maybe one not so rough. He should have checked the cabriolet before he rented it. The next time he took a carriage out, he'd personally inspect every damn wheel himself.

Luke tossed the wheel into the wagon, then stooped to right the carriage. The contraption wasn't heavy, although it was bulky. He maneuvered it to the open end of the wagon, leaned it against the frame to use that as a fulcrum, and lifted the buggy to slide it in. Taking a coil of rope, he started to secure it when his attention was suddenly caught.

He stared for a moment, not quite sure he was seeing what he thought he was seeing. Then he tossed the rope aside and slid his hand along the dangling wooden spindle that had held the wheel in place. Had the bolts simply come loose, causing the wheel to fall off, the spindle should not have broken. Of course, at the rate they were traveling, it could have splintered, causing the wheel to fall off. Instead of ragged edges, though, the hanging piece of wood was smooth.

Like it had been *sawed* part of the way through.

The wheel had not accidently come loose. Someone had deliberately sabotaged the axle, weakening the spindle enough that it would break without too much strain. Which meant that someone had wanted him to get into a serious accident.

No wonder Diablo had acted so high-strung. He'd witnessed the damage being done but couldn't speak English.

And then Luke felt his blood chill. The cabriolet was not his regular carriage. He'd only rented the buggy yesterday afternoon because his own needed maintenance. He'd invited Abby for a ride, and he had parked it beside the general store for about an hour.

Could the carriage have been tinkered with during that time because *Abby* was the one who was supposed to have the accident? Luke recalled the loose step and the incident with the scorpion in the drawer. Were those done on purpose as well?

There was only one person who could have done all of these things.

John.

But the question was *why*. The store's title was in Abby's name now, so barring Luke's own plan for revenge—which was beginning to unravel—John had nothing to gain. He might resent a woman's presence, but she'd let him keep his job. Abby had even told him that once the profits increased, he'd be getting a substantial raise. So why would he want to harm—maybe even kill—her?

It made no sense.

****

"I'm tired of staying in bed." Abby thrust her chin out, knowing she probably looked and sounded like a petulant child.

"The doctor said two days of bed rest," Delia said, pulling the covers up after Abby had pushed them aside. "You've barely had one."

"I have things to do," Abby answered. "The store—"

"Will get along fine without you for a day. Besides, I'm sure Luke will go there later this afternoon."

Abby frowned. "Where is he this morning?"

Delia grinned. "Do you miss him?"

"That's not...*no*, of course not." She didn't sound too sure, even to herself. "That wasn't why I was asking."

"Uh-huh. If you say so." Delia winked.

Abby huffed. Her friend could be *so* persistent. "Well, it's *not*."

"Fine. Actually, he was here this morning."

"He was?" The question was out before Abby could think not to ask. Any interest she showed would only make Delia more dogged in her insistence that romance brewed.

Delia gave her a knowing look. "You were finally asleep. He didn't want to wake you."

It was probably just as well. If the soreness of her cheek was any indication, that side of her face must be a mass of bruises and no doubt turning lovely colors of purple and green by now. Her hair was filthy since she'd landed in dirt, and she needed a hot bath. "Did he leave a message?"

"Only that he was going to go pick up the cabriolet and take it back to the stable." Delia grimaced. "God help the stable owner if there was something wrong with that buggy."

Abby raised a brow on the side of her face that didn't hurt. "Why do you say that?"

"If you could have seen him when he carried you in, you wouldn't have to ask." Delia smiled. "He was nearly beside himself, shouting orders like a Union general and kicking your door open before anyone could get to it."

Abby shifted her gaze to the door. "He kicked it in?"

"Luckily, it wasn't latched. Mrs. Bartlett wouldn't have been happy if he'd torn it off its hinges."

"I doubt he'd do that."

"You didn't see him. He was like a wild animal until the physician finally got here." Delia shook her head. "I'd say that man cares for you a whole lot more than he's willing to let on."

Abby felt a warmth spread through her. Was it possible that he did? She hadn't dared hope the kiss they'd shared had meant as much to him as it did to her. He'd probably kissed scores of women. But what if...

"You're blushing," Delia teased.

"I'm *not*."

Delia arched a brow. "Want a mirror?"

"I'd probably only scare myself."

"You are rather mottled." Her friend sobered. "You really are lucky you weren't killed. I don't think I've ever seen two men as upset as Luke and Ben were."

Abby attempted a smile. "I woke to them arguing."

"I think because they both felt helpless."

"Helpless?" Abby had a hard time fathoming Luke *ever* feeling helpless, and she knew her brother. He'd never admit to feeling vulnerable. If he thought her accident was his fault... She frowned. "By the way, where is Ben?"

"I'm not sure. After breakfast he disappeared. Said he'd be back later." Delia brightened as they heard the front door slam below. "That might be him now. Should I go find out?"

Abby was about to say Ben could find his way to her room, but then she noticed the hopeful expression on Delia's face. It reminded her of her own sense of anticipation when she knew she'd be seeing Luke. She couldn't fault her friend for that feeling.

"You might as well." She'd hardly gotten the sentence out before Delia was striding through the doorway. Abby shook her head. Even though she'd tried to warn her friend that Ben wasn't the type to settle down, she had a feeling she'd have more luck trying to stop a locomotive with an engine full of steam.

She just hoped the train wouldn't crash…although she wasn't sure if she was thinking of Delia just then or herself.

****

By early evening, Abby had had all she could take of lying abed. Ben hadn't returned by the time Delia brought tea and biscuits up earlier, and Abby was a bit disgruntled that Luke hadn't put in an appearance either, but at least she'd been able to take a bath. Although she was stiff and sore and had a myriad of multicolored bruises everywhere, being clean made her feel that she would live.

She was just about to go down for supper when she heard boots coming up the stairs, followed by a brief knock on her door before it swung open. Her brother stood in the doorway with an unreadable expression on his face.

"What is it?" she asked, quickly pulling him inside to shut the door. "Is Luke all right?"

Ben sharpened his gaze. "You're not falling for him, are you?"

She hoped her bruises would cover the blush she felt. "Don't be silly. I just haven't heard from him all day. I thought he might let me know about the buggy."

"Don't know about that. He wasn't at the store when I went by there a little while ago."

"Had John seen him?"

Ben shrugged. "I didn't ask."

Abby refrained from rolling her eyes. Typical male response. Not bothering to find out the details. But she dared not chide him about it, since he already suspected she had a personal interest.

"What have you been doing all day?"

"That's what I came up to talk to you about."

Abby studied him. Ben looked as serious as she'd ever seen him, even the day he was sentenced to prison. Her nape began to prickle. "There *is* something wrong. What aren't you telling me?"

Her brother hesitated. "Luke Cameron isn't exactly who he says he is."

Her stomach sank to her feet and she sat down quickly on the edge of the bed. "What…what do you mean?"

Ben closed the distance and sat down beside her. "I spent the day nosing around the Barbary Coast."

Abby frowned. "What were you doing in that area? I thought you were going to stay away from saloons and dance halls and gambling dens."

"It's a great place to get information," Ben answered.

"What kind of information were you looking for? I know you don't like Luke—"

"It's not that." Ben grimaced. "I've just had a feeling that something wasn't right. He doesn't come across like a banker type."

"He never said he was in banking."

"Maybe not, but when you described how quick he was with his gun, it got me to thinking. And that got me to asking questions."

A part of Abby wanted to bury her head under the pillow and refuse to listen to any more. Another part couldn't stand not knowing. "So…what did you find out?"

"He's a gunslinger."

"Just because he shoots fast? This is the West, Ben.

A lot of cowboys can do that."

Her brother shook his head. "He's a gun-for-hire."

She stared at him. "How do you know that? I doubt saloon patrons are the most reliable sources of information."

"I didn't just take their word. I spent most of the day sending telegrams and waiting for answers."

"To whom?"

"I have my sources." Ben smiled tightly. "You learn a lot spending two years in prison."

"Good Lord, Ben. You're associating with criminals?"

"Are you forgetting we're criminals too?"

"Were. *Were*. Not anymore." She grabbed him. "I don't want you getting back into that."

"I'm not. Don't worry." Ben gently pried her fingers from his arm. "Let's just say the wardens owed me a couple of favors."

At least that was the other side of the law, but she didn't really want to go into that either. "So what did these telegrams say?"

"He's established somewhat of a reputation across Missouri and Kansas," Ben said. "Pinkerton's even hired him on a couple of occasions."

"The detective agency?"

"Yep. And there's an operative right here in San Francisco. I couldn't get him to admit he knew anything, but his pretty little female clerk certainly acknowledged Luke had been in the office just this afternoon."

Abby could just imagine how her charming brother managed to get that information out of the girl, but she wasn't going to ask. She couldn't imagine why Luke would have even gone there. Her throat suddenly felt dry and she swallowed hard. "That still doesn't prove anything."

Ben paused. "There was a witness to Travis Sayer's shooting. A man in the crowd saw Luke pull his gun. A second later, Travis fell to the ground."

"No." Abby shook her head in disbelief. "That couldn't be."

"Why not?"

"Because…" She searched for an answer. "Well, if someone saw Luke do it, why didn't he turn him in?"

Ben shrugged again. "Like you said, this is the West. Men tend to mind their own business."

She knew that was true. It wasn't that much different from the Bowery. An unwritten code of seeing nothing and hearing nothing kept a lot of people alive. "But why would Luke shoot his own cousin?"

"I doubt they were related at all."

"*What*?" This just kept getting worse and worse. "He had a letter from Travis."

Her brother gave her a pitying look, one generally reserved for the dimwitted.

"He *did*. I read it. Travis wanted to expand the store—"

"Luke's not an investor."

"What makes you say that? I admit none of this gun-for-hire stuff makes sense, but that doesn't mean Luke can't be interested in investing."

"It's a scam."

"*What*?" Her hearing must be going or her brother had gone mad. Or maybe she'd hit her head harder than she thought when she flew from the carriage.

Ben took her hand, something he rarely did. "Luke's been talking up this scheme in the gambling dens. He's hinted there might be room for a silent partner to take care of the widows' 'investments.' "

It was a good thing she was sitting, because she suddenly was too weak to stand. She felt as though the world had suddenly dropped out from under her and she was floating mindlessly in air. Luke was an imposter? He'd been lying to her all along?

Suddenly, it made sense why he didn't want her to be any part of the "investment." He never intended to build the expansion and he wanted to keep the money to himself. How could she have been so stupid as not to see it?

How could she have been so stupid?

Chapter Fifteen

Delia told Luke that Abby was sleeping when he stopped by. He didn't want to disturb her. He knew she needed to rest, but he hadn't anticipated how much he was looking forward to seeing her and how oddly disappointed he was that he could not. They needed to talk. About *everything*. Mainly he needed to tell her the real reason he'd come to San Francisco. He'd come clean about it all and pray she'd understand and forgive him. Ferreting out the money-laundering accomplice who'd taken his grandmother's savings was no longer his priority. Finding out why John wanted Abby gone was.

Before he confronted the bastard, though, he needed to make sure he'd taken care of any excuse the man could make. His first stop was the stables where he'd rented the buggy.

Mr. Anderson, the owner, came out as he approached with the wagon. He looked at the cabriolet lying on its side in the bed. "You had an accident?"

"Not exactly," Luke said as he jumped down from the bench. "Sabotage, more likely."

Mr. Anderson's eyes widened. "What do you mean?"

"I'm saying the axle was partially sawed through."

"That's impossible."

Luke studied him, checking for any telltale sign of deceit, but Anderson looked him directly in the eye, his voice was steady, and he wasn't making any nervous movements. Not that Luke had expected anything, but he wanted to rule out any alibis. He gestured. "See for yourself."

The man scrambled onto the wagon bed. It didn't take him long at inspecting the buggy before his face drained of color. "I swear this wasn't the condition I rented it out in."

"Can you be sure?" Luke asked as Anderson climbed down. "Is there any possibility the last renter brought it back like this?"

He shook his head emphatically. "I always inspect the equipment myself when it comes back and again before I rent it out."

Luke was fairly certain the man spoke the truth since he kept all his tack in good condition. Still, another question or two wouldn't hurt.

"Is there any possibility that someone may have tampered with it after you'd done your inspection? Was there anyone about before I picked it up two days ago?"

"No. I looked everything over the night before and locked up the carriage room myself. You were the first client that morning." Anderson gave him a quick perusal. "Thank God you weren't hurt."

"I wasn't," Luke said grimly, "but the lady riding with me was thrown out when the wheel came off."

Anderson's face blanched again. "Did she... Is she all right?"

"She survived. By the way, you might want to leave the buggy as it is in case the constable wants to have a look."

Anderson nodded. "I'll lock it in the carriage house."

"Do that." Luke turned to leave. He hadn't made a report to the authorities yet, but he wanted the evidence waiting when he did. He still had another stop to make.

"My father is in," Isabella said when he arrived at the Pinkerton office right after lunch. "I'll announce you."

"Not necessary." She looked slightly affronted, but he just didn't have time to stand on ceremony. At least not today. He gave her one of his best smiles. "I'll just tell him I barged in."

She looked heavenward, but then relented and smiled back. "Get on with you then."

He stopped smiling when he stepped inside the office and closed the door. Isabella's father looked up from a paper he was studying and then shoved it aside. "You look like you're loaded for bear." He raised a brow. "I thought gunslingers were usually cool and collected."

The man was right. Luke always controlled his emotions. He couldn't afford not to. Reacting, instead of staying in command, could be deadly. Somehow, thinking logically and calmly had become impossible when it came to Abby.

"I need the agency's help."

The brow arched a bit higher. "What's the problem?"

When Luke finished telling him what had transpired and what his suspicions were, the other man nodded. "I'll delve into this John's background and see what I can come up with. Give me a few days."

"Thanks." Luke stood to leave. He wasn't sure he wanted to wait a few days, but there wasn't much choice. He knew these things took time. Meanwhile, he would stick close to Abby like a bee to its honeycomb.

He spent the rest of the afternoon doing some digging on his own, but to no avail. By the time he decided to call it a day, the sun was sinking low on the horizon. It occurred to him that maybe he had been dragging his heels in returning to the boarding house. As much as he wanted to see Abby, he also knew he would be facing a battle much worse than any gunslinger he'd had to face down.

"What do you mean, Abby can't see me?" he asked Ben a short time later when her brother met him in the parlor. "Has she gotten worse?" He jumped up from the chair where he'd been waiting and started to the door. "Did you call the physician?"

Ben blocked him. "Abby's fine."

"If she's fine, then I need to talk to her."

"She doesn't want to talk to you."

Luke stared at him. "Why not?"

Ben glared back. "You should know."

"Damnation! I should know *what*? I have to talk to her!"

Delia emerged from the hall to stand near Ben. "I think you've done enough damage."

He gave her a startled look. "Damage? I can prove the buggy was sab—"

"The buggy has nothing to do with it," Delia said flatly. "You made Abby cry, you deceitful man. You made my friend cry!"

"Cry? Abby cried?" And suddenly, his belly clenched and he felt like he'd swallowed a hot coal. Had he been found out? Before he had a chance to tell her himself? One look at her brother's smug face gave him his answer.

"Get out of my way!" he bellowed and pushed past

Ben, knocking him against the wall. Delia's screech barely registered as he took the stairs three at a time. He wasn't about to lose Abby. Not now when he realized he loved her.

****

Abby jumped out of her dressing chair as the door crashed open and banged against the wall. She gasped when she saw Luke and then turned quickly away before he could see her red, swollen eyes. She didn't hear him approach, but seconds later, his hands were on her shoulders, turning her around.

"Why have you been crying?"

"I—"

"Take your hands off her!" Ben shouted, storming into the room, Delia not far behind.

The lightning-fast reflexes Abby had seen the night of the accident came into play again. Luke spun and ducked as Ben's fist punched past his shoulder, then barreled into him, throwing him off balance. Unfortunately, Abby hadn't moved at all, stunned by what was happening. A second later, she felt a sharp pain as her brother's misguided fist clipped her cheekbone, and she reeled backwards.

Delia screamed while Luke and Ben uttered a string of curses.

Luke caught her and set her on the bed, keeping one arm around her for support.

Ben rushed over. "I'll take care of my sister."

Luke's wolf-colored eyes fixed on him as though he were prey. "I think you've done enough damage."

"Christ! I didn't mean to." Ben sat down beside Abby. "I'm sorry, Sis. Please forgive me. *Please*. I never meant to hit you."

"I know you didn't," Abby said, wincing as she touched her cheek.

"Go see if the landlady has some ice or a raw beefsteak." Luke glowered at Ben. "Either will keep the swelling down."

"I'll do it," Delia said and fled down the stairs.

"Christ," Ben said again, looking miserable. "I meant to hit *him*, not you."

Luke's gaze hardened. "If it's a fight you're looking for, that can be arranged."

Ben glared back. "Just name the time and place."

"Stop it! Both of you." Abby closed her eyes against the sharp, searing pain. "You're both acting like schoolboys."

"I am not."

"Neither am I."

She opened her eyes slowly. "You *sound* like schoolboys, too."

Luke growled and Ben huffed, but they both remained silent. She would have rolled her eyes, but she had a feeling the movement would hurt. Luckily, Delia returned with a bowl of ice and a washcloth.

"Mrs. Bartlett says she wants no fighting in her house."

"Nobody's going to fight anybody," Abby said as her brother and Luke scowled at each other. She gave each of them a look out of her good eye. "Am I right?"

"I suppose," Ben muttered.

"For now, anyway," Luke added as he wrapped some of the ice in the washcloth and held it to Abby's face.

The cold felt like heaven, or maybe it was Luke's touch that numbed the pain. But a look at Ben's face made her realize that the simple gesture was riling his temper again, and inwardly she sighed. "I can hold the pack in place."

For a moment, she didn't think Luke was going to let go, but then he pressed her hand against the cloth and dropped his. "Move it around a little so your skin doesn't freeze."

She nodded. "Now that truce has been declared, why are you here, Luke?"

"We need to talk." He glanced at Ben and Delia, then turned back. "In private."

Ben crossed his arms. "I'm not leaving you alone with my sister in her bedroom."

"Damnation, she's hurt," Luke replied. "I'm hardly going to take advantage of her."

"Not moving," Ben answered.

"Me either," Delia chimed in. "I'll be the chaperone or…" She grinned cheekily. "…the referee, if needed."

Abby recognized the look on her brother's face. Even if she could get him—and Delia—to leave, he'd just listen at the door. She turned to Luke. "You might as well say what you came to say."

He sighed. "Why were you crying?"

Ben narrowed his eyes. "You know damn well—"

"I'm asking Abby."

She kept her eyes down, then swallowed hard, praying she wouldn't start crying again. "You deceived me, Luke." When he didn't answer, she looked up. "You aren't going to deny it?"

He shook his head. "It's true. But…" He held up his hand before anyone could speak. "I had a reason that had nothing to do with you. If you'll give me just a few minutes of your time, I'll explain." He took a deep breath. "And then I'll leave—for good—if you want me to."

Dear Lord. She should just tell him to go, but blast it, she knew she didn't want him to leave. As upset as she was, as hurt as she felt, she didn't want him to go. Not *for good.* She was a fool for caring, but she did. She more than cared. She'd let herself fall in love with him, and that's why his deception cut to her core. She must be a real glutton for punishment.

"Tell me."

Her brother started to sputter, but she cut him off. "Please, Ben. I need to hear this from Luke."

"Fine." He gave Luke a black look. "But if you make my sister cry—"

"He won't." Abby lifted her chin, determined to make her words true.

"Thank you," Luke said. "It all started with my grandmother—"

"Your *grandmother?*" Of all the things she'd expected to come out of his mouth, none of them had to do with his grandmother.

He nodded and continued. By the time he finished explaining how he'd wanted to get his grandmother's money back by setting up his own scheme, and that he'd decided to abandon the plan and return all the widows' investment money, she could only stare at him.

"What made you change your mind?" she asked. He hesitated so long she didn't think he was going to answer.

"You," he finally said.

"Me?"

"Yes. I…" He paused again and looked at his intrigued audience of two, then turned back to Abby.

"All your hopes and dreams are tied up in making the store successful. I didn't want to be the one to bring your world crashing down."

She had a feeling he'd meant to say something else, but she didn't know what that would be. Still, the words he did say warmed her heart. He must care, at least a little.

"There's something else you should know," he said.

"There's *more*?" Was he actually going to *say* he cared?

"I'm the one who killed your fiancé." He took a deep breath. "I shot Travis Sayer."

For a moment, Abby could only stare. So it was true what Ben had said.

"You're a gunslinger." Ben took a step forward. "Were you hired to kill him?"

"My gun has been for hire, but those days are in my past." Luke shook his head. "I never shot to kill unless it was absolutely unavoidable. And I didn't come here to kill Sayer. I wanted my grandmother's money back."

Abby furrowed her brows. "Then why did you shoot him?"

He sighed. "I only meant to wound him so he'd stop dragging that dance hall girl down the street. Someone jostled my arm just as I pulled the trigger. Believe me when I say I wanted him alive."

"I suppose that would have been to your advantage." Abby slid a glance to Ben first, then took a deep breath. "I have a confession to make as well."

"*Don't*," Ben warned. "You don't owe him any confessions."

"But he's being honest with us," Abby replied. "He should know—"

"*No. Don't*," Ben said again. "He doesn't need to—
"

"—know that both of you were pickpockets in New York?" Luke asked.

Ben's mouth dropped open and Abby turned startled eyes to Luke. "You *know*?"

"Have for quite a while."

"*Criminy*! You never said a word."

"Well, I had my secrets, so I thought you were entitled to yours."

"If that don't beat all," Delia said suddenly. "There's been a drama unfolding right here with more secrets than that *Hamlet* play I saw." She gave them a mischievous grin. "But I'm not sure all the secrets are out." She looked from Abby to Luke. "Are they?"

Chapter Sixteen

"Mmmm." Abby rolled over in bed and burrowed into Luke's welcoming embrace. She nuzzled contentedly into the crevice between arm and shoulder, preparing to drift deeper into sleep.

"That's it," he murmured as he tilted her head slightly so he could brush feather kisses along the slim column of her neck. "Do you like this?"

"Mmmm," she mumbled again. What an exquisite dream. She was lying against Luke's hard length, his body heat warming her to her toes. His hand stroked down her ribs and over her hips while his breath fanned her cheek as he gently nibbled at her ear. She felt weightless, boneless, almost un-embodied except for everywhere he touched. Those places tingled as though she sat too close to a fire. A finger lifted her chin and she felt his lips slip lightly across hers, teasing her into wanting more. She wrapped her arms around his neck and moaned softly as he deepened the kiss...

And suddenly, she was wide awake. The curtains fluttered by the open window, the dim light from the street lamp below reflecting shadowy shapes. But she didn't need the light to know that she was not alone in her bed.

Her reactive jerk must have alerted him, because he placed a hand over her mouth before she could scream. "Shhhh. You'll wake everyone."

Luke. Luke? No dream, then. He was really here. Abby tugged at his hand and he slowly removed it. "Shhhh," he said again.

She looked toward the door. She had bolted it before she went to bed and it was still closed. She doubted he could have snuck up the stairs anyway, since they creaked and groaned like crazy. "How did you get in here?"

He motioned to the open window. "There's a trellis outside."

"That rickety old thing? It's a wonder you didn't fall to your death."

"It's only two stories," he replied. "And I've climbed much worse."

Natural curiosity arose and she wanted to ask, but perhaps this wasn't the best time, given the circumstances. "What exactly are you doing here?"

"I wanted to finish our conversation from earlier." Luke sat up and reached for the oil lamp on the bedside table. In a few seconds, a soft, yellow glow filled the room.

Abby blinked as her eyes adjusted to the brightness. At least they were both still clothed. Sort of. His black shirt was half-open, revealing his broad chest. Its sleeves were rolled up, baring muscular forearms. His dark hair was tousled and the angle at which he was sitting on the edge of the bed cast half his face into silhouette, giving him an otherworldly, predatory look. Her every nerve ending tingled, but not from fear of having a dangerous-looking man in her bedroom. Her body wanted him back in her bed. Back in her dream...only it hadn't been a dream.

She pushed herself into a sitting position against the

headboard. "Our conversation?"

"The one we were having in front of an audience."

Abby frowned. "I thought we'd cleared the air. You know my past. I know you wanted to force the sale of the store but changed your mind. You have another confession?" Her frown deepened. "Or did you lie?"

"Yes."

She strove to keep her voice calm. "Which? Confession or lie?"

"Both." Luke hesitated. "I lied—a little bit—when I said I'd changed my mind because the store meant so much to you. I mean, that's the truth, but it isn't the reason. Exactly."

She furrowed her brows again, this time in confusion. "You aren't making any sense. You didn't fall from the trellis on a first attempt, did you?"

"I didn't fall." Then he smiled lopsidedly. "Well, maybe I did."

"Maybe? You should know if you fell." His smile looked rather strange. "Maybe you hit your head like I did?"

"No." He sighed. "I'm making a mess of this."

For the first time since she'd known him, he looked at a loss. She wanted to tell him to just say whatever it was he wanted to say, but she had the distinct feeling he'd spout more gibberish. He was already studying the pattern on the wallpaper as if it might have some significance, although it was mostly just leaves and entwined vines. So she simply folded her hands across the bed sheet and waited while he continued to peruse the foliage.

"I love you," he suddenly blurted.

Abby blinked. Was Luke addressing the wallpaper?

She didn't think the pattern was all that fascinating, herself, but maybe his grandmother had the same one. Then again, maybe she'd only thought that was what he said. Her mind really wanted to drift back to that very nice dream...er, not a dream, but...

"I love you." This time Luke looked directly at her. "That was the confession I wanted to make. I decided to drop my plans because I love you."

Abby's mouth opened, but no sound came out. She tried again, but only emitted something very close to a sick frog's *ribbit*.

"You don't have to say anything." He took a deep breath. "I just wanted you to know."

She managed something that sounded like the squeak of a mouse.

"Right." Luke moved toward the window. "I'll be leaving then."

"Don't take another step!" She regained her voice. "Not. One. More. Step."

Luke stopped and raised an eyebrow. "Was there something you wanted to say?"

"*Criminy.*"

The brow arched a bit higher. "I'm not sure what that means."

At the moment, she wasn't sure either. She just knew that her anticipation—the hopes and desires she'd tried to suppress because she thought there was no point—were all bubbling to the surface like a kettle left on the stove for too long. Her emotions were all colliding, about to boil over. Luke loved her! And then she realized he was watching her with a puzzled look on his face. She hadn't answered him and she didn't even have the excuse of studying the wallpaper. "Criminy."

"You've already said that. Translation, please?"

Giddiness threatened to erupt, but she managed to tamp the feeling. "Forget that word. Here's the important one. Love. I *love* you too, Luke."

His eyes darkened to a cognac color. "Do you mean that?"

"Of course I do."

He moved toward the bed. "Tomorrow. I'll talk to Ben tomorrow and tell him he'll be seeing a lot more of me."

"That should go over well."

"Doesn't matter." Luke's eyes darkened. "But for tonight, perhaps we can seal our feelings with a kiss? A real one?"

"Just a kiss?" Abby lifted the sheet and patted the bed. "I'd like to finish that dream we started."

Luke grinned. "So would I."

Abby smiled back. "Then I'd suggest you remove your clothes."

He didn't need to be told twice. She didn't think she'd ever seen someone disrobe so quickly. Not that she'd ever seen a man disrobe. She hadn't even see Ben naked since they were both small enough for their mother to give them baths. She couldn't help the gasp that escaped her lips when Luke was free of his Levis and she saw how big his...*thing*...was. She did know where it was supposed to go. "It'll never fit."

Luke chuckled. "Believe me, darlin'. It will fit."

She was about to argue the point when her speech was cut off by his mouth closing over hers. There was nothing light or teasing about this kiss. Instead, his lips were firm and warm, his tongue demanding entrance. With a soft mewl, she opened to him, her own tongue doing battle.

He groaned and deepened the kiss while one hand palmed a breast, kneading it gently before the rough callus of his thumb swept across the nipple. Immediately, it budded, and she gasped again as he flicked the hard tip, over and over. His mouth left hers to trail kisses down her neck and across her collarbone while his hand tended her now heavy, aching breast. And then she started as his tongue swirled around the aureole of the other one, causing it to peak as well. The pleasure was near unbearable and she arched her back instinctively, wanting more friction. She heard a rumble deep in his throat and then he pulled the nipple into his mouth and began to suckle, lightly at first and then harder. Sensation pierced her body, sending quivers of delight coursing through her. An odd throbbing began between her legs and she felt herself grow damp.

And his hands were everywhere, like molten lava, heating every part of her that he touched. Her ribs, her abdomen, her hips…sliding down her thighs and then *up* to the juncture where they met. She gasped again as his fingers separated her slick folds, and she nearly came off the bed when he rubbed the sensitive little nub.

"Criminy!"

He looked up. "I am definitely going to learn the meaning of that word."

He could speak rationally when she could scarcely *think*? Especially when his clever fingers had not stopped what they were doing. He was going to drive her mad.

"Er…ah…you… Arrgh!" Whatever he was doing, she had lost any coherent ability.

"You like that?" he asked.

What a stupid question. As if he couldn't tell. Before

she could gather enough wits to say that, he'd changed position. Suddenly her legs were spread wide as he knelt between them, her knees over his shoulders. She was completely vulnerable and fully exposed to him. "What….are…you…doing?"

"Just this." And then he dipped his head.

If she'd thought his fingers were magic, the feeling of his tongue lapping at her and then licking its way slowly up her folds took what tiny bit of sense remained in her brain. All she felt was sensation. Every nerve was on fire, but at the same time all feeling was concentrated *there*. His hands slid up to knead her breasts once more, his thumbs grazing her nipples, as he drew her wildly throbbing nub into his mouth and sucked hard.

Abby came undone. All that mattered was the sensation building, bubbling, boiling like a volcano about to erupt as Luke slowed to leisurely nibbling and licking her core while he pulled and tugged at her nipples. And then he sucked hard once more and Abby exploded. Colored lights swirled around her and she floated senselessly in the air like so much ash before gradually descending to reality.

She had barely opened her eyes when she felt his big member nudging at her opening. Except it didn't feel so huge anymore. She was all soft and pliant, and the feeling of him filling her as he plunged his full length into her felt like heaven. Her nub started throbbing again as he began thrusting, and soon another crest began to build. Her belly clenched hard as he drove himself harder and deeper. She felt herself contract around him and felt something hot spurt inside her. The last thing she heard was him saying, "I told you it would fit"…and then the lights sparkled once more, sending her into oblivion.

****

Luke reined in Diablo behind the store and dismounted. The hours since he'd left Abby in exhausted sleep had seemed like an eternity, yet at the same time flashed by mainly because he could think of nothing else besides her. He'd relived their lovemaking—all four times—so often that his shaft had stayed permanently hard when it should have been taking a well-deserved rest.

Abby was quite the lover. He'd been pleasantly surprised—and maybe a little smug—to discover she was a virgin. Not that it mattered except he felt honored to have been the first to introduce her to the pleasures of bed sport.

And he would also be the *last* man to do so. He had intended to meet with her brother this morning and declare his intention to marry Abby, but she had asked him to wait. She said Ben needed time to absorb all that had been said yesterday afternoon, and their sudden engagement would only make him think Luke was using her. He didn't much like the idea, but he could see her point. He was going to have to win Ben's trust first.

One of the things he had discussed with Abby— while they had enough energy left to talk—was how to ease John out of his job. Luke had shared his suspicions that John was behind the accidents because he didn't want Abby running the store, but to fire him without cause might bring retaliation. Better to find a reason to let him go. Before that, though, they needed a thorough knowledge of the physical end of the business. It meant checking the incoming inventory personally, meeting with vendors, and even the *Neptune Maiden*'s captain…chores that John had done before. Once he was gone, Luke wanted operations to continue to run smoothly.

He grinned as he climbed the back steps to the store. He had every intention of *personal* operations concerning Abby to run smoothly as well…like a ship sailing at high tide with full sails.

****

"That's the schooner that brings you the goods from the East?" Ben asked Abby as they stood on the docks watching the *Neptune Maiden* putting into port two days later. A number of dock-handlers stood ready to throw lines or receive them, depending on which of the giant cleats were next to each man that would secure the ship to the pier.

"Yes. I hardly ever get to see her come in, since she usually arrives at night," Abby replied. "So this is a surprise."

"She's got sleek lines." Ben squinted his eyes against the sun. "Ships have always fascinated me."

Abby was surprised. "I didn't know that."

Ben grinned. "Remember when I used to play hooky from school?"

"I doubt I'd forget. The nuns practically put me through the Inquisition about where you might be."

"Um, well. I suppose they felt obligated to try to keep their sheep in one flock."

Abby shook her head. "Like you were ever a sheep. You never would follow anyone's lead."

"I didn't want anyone telling me what to do." Ben shrugged. "Still don't."

She gave him a wary look. "I meant what I said about staying retired from our old ways."

"And I told you I would."

Abby decided it might be best not to push the subject. "So—just curious—where *did* you go when you played hooky?"

He grinned again. "I'd sneak over to the Hudson River and watch the boats and barges. Mostly, I liked to think about where the big ships were going when they left the docks."

Abby frowned. "Did you want to leave on one of them?"

"Well, we didn't exactly have a life of luxury. Adventure sounded like a good alternative." Ben looked down at her. "Didn't you want to get away?"

"I guess I never thought about it much," Abby replied. "Mother needed us."

"That's why we did what we did." He was quiet for a moment and then he smiled. "But you *did* get away after all. You came all the way out West on your own. I found it to be almost as much an adventure as sailing to parts unknown."

"I didn't think of it as an adventure. I just needed a place to start over. This was the best opportunity." Abby shook her head. "You really are a romantic."

Ben studied her. "Do you think you would have learned to love Sayer if he'd lived?"

Abby felt a twinge of guilt that she hadn't really given it much thought, and maybe a second twinge knowing that Luke was the person who'd shot him, albeit not intentionally. She'd never had the chance to meet Travis, so perhaps her apathy had some logic. His few letters had been polite. She'd been aware of what marriage involved and had been willing to do her duty—anything was worth getting away from her former life—but whether she'd ever develop feelings for him? She lifted a shoulder and let it drop. "He was already dead when I arrived, so I'll never know."

"My ever-practical sister." Ben gave her a sideways glance. "What about Cameron?"

She started, hoping her face wasn't going to turn pink. She wasn't quite ready to tell Ben about that relationship yet. "What about him?"

He laughed. "Have you forgotten that being observant is what made us successful pickpockets?"

"Shhh!" She looked around, although there wasn't anyone near enough to hear. "That subject is not open for discussion."

"All right," Ben said affably. "So what about Cameron?"

"I have no comment."

Ben raised a brow. "My eyes tell me a different story. The looks you give each other could ignite a fire on wet wood."

Forget pink. From the way her cheeks burned, she was probably the color of a beet. "I don't know what you mean."

"You're losing your acting skills, little sister." Her brother narrowed his eyes. "You've both been acting funny the last couple of days."

"Don't be silly." She turned her attention back to the ship, watching as a number of barrels were unloaded. Better to redirect the conversation to the ship. If Ben had any idea of the lovemaking she'd already shared with Luke, or how the memory of it remained clear as a mountain stream, he would force Luke to marry her. Or worse, call him out. And she'd seen Luke in action with a gun. She had to make sure Ben didn't suspect.

Perhaps her "acting skills" were better than her

brother knew.

****

Abby tossed and turned in bed that evening, unable to fall asleep. Partly because she wanted Luke to "visit" again and partly because she was afraid Ben would catch them. Frustrating as it was, they had to move slowly and give her brother time to absorb the change taking place.

She finally gave up, threw the covers back, and went to the window. It was a clear night and she could see the streets were quiet and empty, which meant it was probably well after midnight. Her thoughts turned back to the events of the day. She'd had no idea Ben was so interested in ships. And, he had given her a new perspective on the *Neptune Maiden*. She'd simply thought of it as a cargo ship, but Ben had pointed out she was built for speed, more like a warship than a freighter. Which made her wonder why the schooner was being used for transport.

The crew was certainly skilled at unloading the ship. The contents had been quickly put into three wagons that John had sent down to the docks, and he had shown up to supervise the loading, a job that Ben was probably going to have to learn once they let John go.

Then she frowned as she remembered the barrels in the last wagon. They were smaller than the pickle and grain barrels used in the store. And lighter in color, although she supposed if they were coming from the Orient, they might be bamboo. Still, she'd never seen them on the floor. Was John possibly purchasing some goods that weren't used in the store but they were being charged for?

She began to pace. Both Luke and Ben had agreed it would be easier—or at least justifiable—if they could find something fraudulent with how John ran the store. Ben had already started double-checking past invoices against inventory. Luke was going to request copies of the bills-of-lading the *Neptune Maiden*'s captain would have given the shipper in India, but that would take a little time.

Maybe the shipment of barrels was listed on the new invoice. John would have it and she could look tomorrow. But before they could accuse John of anything, they needed physical evidence. That meant they needed to take a look at those barrels. What was in them?

The more she thought about it, the more inquisitive she became. And the more restless. She doubted she'd be getting any sleep. Abby eyed the cape she'd left lying on the chair. She had a set of Ben's clothing in her trunk. It had come in handy at times in the Bowery when she wanted to move about unnoticed. Maybe she should go to the store now, in the wee hours when no one was about, and see for herself what the contents were. That way, she'd know if they had any evidence of wrongdoing before talking to John.

She changed into her boyish costume and put on sturdy walking shoes. For a moment she contemplated waking her brother, then decided against it. He could be like a bear awakened during hibernation when his sleep was disturbed. She could go, check out the barrels, and be back in less than an hour. Having made up her mind, she pulled the cape over her shoulders and slipped out.

From living in the Bowery, she knew that this late— or early—the drunks would be sleeping off the effects and the street gangs would be home, the streets clear, so she was surprised to see a horse and small, open cart in front of the store at this hour. Abby glanced in the display window, but all was dark within. She didn't see anyone near the horse, and the cart was empty. Who in the world would be parked here? And why?

She inched closer to the side of the building, then flattened herself against the wood as she spotted movement. It took only a moment before John walked out of the shadows, carrying one of the barrels from the ship. Another man, one she'd never seen before, followed him with a second barrel to place in the cart. She moved quickly to stand behind a tree so they wouldn't see her when they turned around. It looked like John was indeed stealing part of the inventory that had been brought in this afternoon. It seemed she had the proof she needed.

Suddenly, she heard a footstep crunch on the gravel behind her. She turned, just in time to see a cloaked figure stepping from the shadows as something was thrown over her head. And then, she couldn't breathe.

Chapter Seventeen

Wild banging on his hotel door jarred Luke awake from a wonderful dream of being in bed with Abby and having her writhing beneath him. Lucifer's horns! Whoever it was would break the hinges in another minute. He grabbed the six-shooter he kept by his bed, even though his still dream-logged brain was telling him an assassin would hardly bother to knock.

Grabbing a towel, he wrapped it around himself and unlocked the door.

"Where is she?" Ben pushed past him, fists clenched as he glanced at the slept-in empty bed. Then he looked around. "Where is she?"

Luke blinked. "What are you talking about?"

"Don't think you can hide what you're doing from me. I ought to kill you right now."

Luke looked at his gun. "I think I have the advantage on you."

Ben ignored him as he walked to the wardrobe and threw the double doors open. Then he glared at Luke. "Abby's not here."

"Of course she's not…" His addled, still-lust-filled mind finally cleared. "Abby's missing?"

Ben gave him a suspicious look. "You really don't know where she is?"

"*No.*" He reached for his jeans and started dressing. "When did you find out?"

164

"Less than a half hour ago. I knocked on her door and there was no answer. When I opened it, the room was empty. I came right over here."

Luke finished buttoning his shirt and picked up his pocket fob. Half past seven o'clock. He willed himself to remain calm, like he did facing down an outlaw. "Is there any possibility she went to the store early?"

"At this hour?" Ben shook his head. "We always have breakfast together first."

His senses sharpened, instinct telling him something was very wrong. Somehow, he managed to remain rational. "Was there any sign of a struggle?"

"No. Her bed was unmade, but her night rail was lying across it." Ben's eyes widened. "You think she was abducted?"

Luke considered. "Doubtful, if she got dressed. Someone bent on snatching her wouldn't have given her the time."

For a moment relief flickered over Ben's face, then was gone. "Then where could she be?"

"I suggest we start at the store, even if it is early." He doubted she was there, but they had to start somewhere. "Just one more thing before we go."

Ben paused in mid-stride to the door. "What? We're wasting time."

"I love your sister."

Ben narrowed his eyes. "Does she know?"

Luke nodded. "She feels the same. We're going to get married."

"We can discuss that later."

"We can and will." Luke moved toward the door, his face grim. "But first, we have to find her."

****

Abby slowly awakened to near darkness and complete disorientation. She was lying on a narrow cot, but it was moving, rocking gently like a cradle. Her throat hurt. She put a hand up to touch her neck, then winced at the pain. Had someone tried to strangle her? Her mind began to clear and she remembered going to the store and watching John take barrels from the basement and load them into the cart. Then someone had attacked her from behind and covered her head with some kind of sack. She must have lost consciousness.

She sat up, fighting a wave of dizziness, then realized it was the small room—hardly the size of a closet—that was moving. It swayed from side to side, and she heard boards creaking. It took another moment to realize she must be on a ship. Was it the *Neptune Maiden*? The schooner had brought in the barrels John had taken from the basement. Was it possible the crew or even the captain was involved? It didn't make sense. They surely wouldn't be taking back inventory they'd already unloaded. The ship would probably be sailing at next tide to return to the Orient.

And she would be on it.

The thought made her blood chill and then a second thought made it freeze. She remembered Luke telling her that San Francisco's Barbary Coast shared a horrible history with the pirates of the infamous North African coast…and that sultans preferred blondes.

She was blonde.

And the *Neptune Maiden* traded in the Orient.

Abby jumped up and reached the door in three strides. And found it locked. Not that she'd expected it to be open, but she had to try. She sank back down on the cot and tried to gather her wits. Dear Lord! She couldn't be a captive!

She had no idea what time it was or how long she had been on board. She stilled, straining her ears for any sounds of activity that would indicate they were making ready to be underway. She could hear no shouts, no sounds of men moving about, but she didn't know how far below deck she was.

And how long did she have before the ship sailed?

****

Luke wasn't particularly surprised that all was quiet when they arrived at the store. It was barely eight o'clock and not much stirred in San Francisco before midmorning. But at least John was not here, either, so it would give them time to search without being watched.

He let them inside with his key. Ben looked around. "Everything seems in order here."

"I'll check the office," Luke said, but he hardly expected to find Abby sitting at the desk. She wasn't.

"Do you think she actually came here?" Ben asked.

"Where else would she have gone?" Luke responded.

"I don't know. We all agreed we suspect John had something to do with the accidents and that he doesn't want Abby running the store for some reason. It seems reasonable that Abby would want to investigate when he wasn't around."

"Reasonable? Without telling you?"

"My sister has an independent streak. Once her mind's set…" Ben half-quirked his mouth. "She's stubborn. If you're serious about marrying her, you'd better get used to it."

As if Luke hadn't already noticed her willfulness. Secretly, he thought it a good quality. At least to a point.

Right now, he wished he'd stayed at the boarding house and guarded her door. She would have been furious at finding him there, but at least she wouldn't be missing now. Damn it!

"Let's take a look in the basement before we leave." He kept his tone neutral, but anxiety flared in Ben's eyes.

"You think she might be…hurt?" He didn't wait for an answer as he hurried outside to the side where the cellar door was. Luke was on his heels.

"It's locked. From the outside." Ben said, prodding the padlock holding the doors shut. "I guess she didn't go down there."

"Since we're here, we might as well check it out." Luke produced a second key he'd recently had made. "If nothing's amiss, we'll go report Abby missing to the authorities."

Throwing the doors open, they descended the stone steps into the earth cellar and he lit an oil lamp that hung from a hook. Everything seemed to be in order. Shelves held a variety of dry goods. Workmen's tools were neatly stacked in one corner. Barrels had been stored on wooden pallets to keep rot away.

"Nothing seems to be disturbed," Luke said, not sure if he was disappointed or relieved.

Ben glanced around, then frowned. "I wonder where the small barrels are."

Luke gave him a questioning look. "Small barrels? There's only one size."

"No. Abby and I watched the shipment being unloaded yesterday. There were six smaller, lighter-colored barrels that were put into one of the wagons. John rode in that wagon as they drove here." Ben looked around again. "I don't see them anywhere."

Luke took the lamp off the wall and started inspecting. He stopped near the area next to the tools. "Looks like the dirt here has been scraped. This is probably where they were put down."

Ben came over. "But why would they disappear? If it's part of our inventory—"

"Maybe it's not." Luke frowned. "Maybe John was bringing something in that we didn't know about."

"Like what?"

"I don't know…" Luke knelt and sifted the loosened dirt with his fingers. As he did, he unearthed a sliver of wood. Holding it up to the light, he ran his thumb along one edge. "This is fresh wood. It must have broken off one of the barrels."

"Here's another piece." Ben pushed it with his boot and then pointed. "And what is that over there?"

Luke looked to where Ben had gestured. Something greenish-gray that looked like a small ball had rolled against the wall. He moved to pick it up, then stood so they could both get a better look. "It looks like part of a plant."

Ben put a finger to a crack on the ball and pressed. A sticky fluid oozed out. He rubbed his fingers together, and then his eyes widened. "This is a poppy pod."

Luke drew his brows together. "Are you sure?"

"Pretty sure," Ben answered. "We had a lot of unsavory types in the Bowery. Some of them dealt in opium. When the homeless drunks couldn't get any alcohol, they'd raid the trash for the empty pods and suck on them. They looked just like this one."

"Damnation!" Luke grimaced. "There are opium dens all over Chinatown. I should have suspected something before."

"Opium isn't illegal, though," Ben said.

"But smuggling it in to avoid paying taxes *is*," Luke answered. "And the *Neptune Maiden* makes frequent trips to the Orient."

"You think the captain of the ship is aware?"

"I don't know. It depends on what the bill-of-lading said was in the barrels," Luke replied, "but the ship puts into Victoria first, where they don't have to pay taxes. Smuggling goods in from Canada is big business here."

"I guess that answers the question about what John's been up to and why he doesn't want Abby to find out," Ben said.

"But it doesn't answer what happened to Abby." Luke's gut burned suddenly. "I don't have a good feeling about this."

"You think something's happened to Abby." Ben made it sound more like a statement than a question.

Luke nodded. "I think we'd better have another look around outside."

It didn't take very long for them to notice where the gravel had been disturbed near the oak tree in front of the store, like there might have been some kind of scuffle. Then Luke's eye caught a piece of plaid fabric stuck to the rough trunk. He pulled it loose.

"Abby's shirt. Mine, actually," Ben said numbly. "She wears it when she disguises herself as a boy."

Luke didn't have time to ask what that meant. She'd been abducted. Luke pulled the watch fob out of his pocket. "High tide is in one hour."

"You think she's been taken to the schooner?" Ben asked.

"It stands to reason. If she caught John removing the barrels…if the captain is in cahoots…" He thrust the bit of fabric at Ben. "Take this to the constable and bring him—and as many men as are available—to the docks. We need to inspect the *Neptune Maiden* before she leaves."

Ben took it. "You're going to the ship?"

Luke nodded grimly. "I'm going to the ship. She isn't sailing without me."

****

Abby was frantic. She could now hear the sounds of preparation for departure. There was no mistaking the clanking and the sounds of metal chain being hauled onboard or the running footsteps above deck and the shouting of orders. They were getting ready to leave.

A key turned in the lock to the cabin. The bright light from the outside as the door opened nearly blinded her. A young sailor stood in the doorway with a loaf of bread and what looked like a wrapped hunk of cheese. "Captain said to bring you this."

"Thank you." She placed the food on the cot and eyed the sailor. He couldn't be much older that herself. "Where is the ship going?"

"Can't say."

Couldn't or wouldn't? She'd have to resort to something else. Abby gave him a smile. "Do you suppose the captain would allow me on deck to watch the ship leaving?"

He shook his head. "It's too dangerous for a lady. Especially one as pretty as you."

She kept her smile pasted on her face as she rose and took the two steps that put her inches away from him. "I'd be safe if you escorted me." He seemed intrigued. "I'd really like to see what is going on."

He shook his head again. "Captain said you were to

stay in the cabin."

She managed to feign innocence. "Am I a prisoner, then?"

He looked uncomfortable. "Can't say."

"Well, I mean, the door was locked." Abby moved slightly closer and rested one hand on the sailor's shoulder. His eyes widened at her touch. "Won't you please let me out for just a few minutes?" She trailed her fingers along the collar of his shirt. "I promise to behave."

He was clearly distracted. For a moment, Abby thought he might even give in. If she could just get on deck… She could pretend to twist an ankle and ask him to go for help. Then she'd make a dash for the gangplank. It would be the last thing to be lifted, since all sailors had to be accounted for before a ship left port. And—she'd thought the procedure terrible when she'd first heard it— ships often took on "unwilling" sailors at the last minute if they needed more crew or if some unscrupulous person wanted to get rid of an enemy. Shanghaied, they called it.

She'd never in the world thought she'd be one of those enslaved captives. Abby squelched the rising panic and leaned forward until she was just brushing against him. "Please? Just five minutes." She gave him the seductive look she'd seen Delia use. At least, she *hoped* it was seductive. *Prayed* that it was. "Then you can bring me back down here."

His eyes darkened. She held her smile in place along with her breath. Would the ruse work? His raised his hand to touch her and then it dropped. He stepped back.

"I'll get in trouble." Without another word, he turned and practically stumbled out of the cabin. A moment later she heard the key turn in the lock.

For a moment, she sagged against the door to collect her thoughts. Then she looked down at her hand. The one that hadn't been stroking his collar. In it lay a small dagger like those all sailors carried.

Ben would have been proud she hadn't lost her skill. Then she pushed the thought aside. Hopefully, her ability to pick a lock was just as good.

She knelt beside the door and stuck the tip of the knife into the lock. Thankfully, it was a standard type that used a skeleton key. It didn't take but a few minutes to push the key out and onto the paper she slipped under the door. Saying a quick prayer of thanks, she pulled the key under the door and picked it up. Then she paused, tuning her ears like a terrier for any noise nearby. Hearing only the sounds up on deck, she took the cap the sailor, in his hurry to exit the cabin, had dropped. Stuffing her hair under it, she opened the door and slipped out.

Freedom was close. Abby stood for a moment to get her bearings. There was a door that appeared to be another cabin beside hers, along with two more across. A ladder led to an open hatch at the end of the narrow passageway, which meant she was probably near the captain's quarters in the stern of the boat. Cautiously, she climbed up and poked her head over the ledge. Just as she thought, sailors and deckhands were moving about, stowing anything loose and securing what needed to stay on deck. She flattened herself against a bulkhead and started to edge to midship where the gangplank was. At least, her men's clothing would let her blend in for the short distance where she could be spotted once she left the shadows and crossed to the gangplank. She hoped.

Trailing one hand along the bulkhead and keeping her head down, she was just a few yards away when someone carrying a big box bumped into her. She lurched sideways. As she did, her cap flew off and her hair tumbled down.

Time stood still as the man stared at her and she stared back. Then he reached for her just as she bolted. He shouted for help. Abby ducked another swipe of a sailor's arm, scrambling and half-crawling toward the plank. Using the dagger, she slashed at a hand reaching for her and then rolled, slashing at another, causing both a howl and a roar of anger. In seconds, she was surrounded, held tightly by both arms while the captain came forward.

"You should have stayed in your cabin, wench." He motioned to his men. "Take her below decks and tie her down this time."

"I wouldn't do that if I were you."

Abby stopped struggling. That voice belonged to only one man. She peered around one of the men hanging on to her and nearly wept with relief.

Luke stood by the rail, pistol pointed at the captain. Below him, on the dock, her brother Ben was closing in with what looked like an army behind him.

Luke gave her a quick glance before returning his wolf-colored gaze to the captain again. His voice was feral when he spoke. "I suggest you release my fiancée."

The captain gestured and the sailors stepped back. Abby rushed to Luke. He tucked her against his side, his gun still trained on the captain as they backed slowly down the gangplank. They had hardly put their feet on the pier when Ben's army of men rushed by to board the ship, where all hell broke loose.

But Abby wasn't watching. Her eyes closed as Luke brought her into his warm embrace and covered her mouth in a long, hot kiss.

Epilogue

Four months later

"I'm glad you decided to keep the ladies' club going," Delia told Abby as they sipped tea—brought by a different ship—and listened to the ladies' friendly boasting about the exotic spice recipes they kept inventing.

"I am too," Abby answered. In truth, she had been afraid, after the arrest of the *Neptune Maiden*'s captain, that they wouldn't be able to find another supplier, but Luke had made inquiries—with a little help from the Pinkerton agency—and found a legitimate importer.

He'd also gathered the widows together and been totally honest about his "scheme," assuring them all of their money would be returned. To Abby's surprise, the women had asked if they couldn't actually go ahead with the plan to expand. They rather liked the idea of investing their own money and having a percentage of profit.

And then, after Luke had announced they were getting married, those ladies went into a true competition frenzy for the best sweets at the reception they insisted on holding.

Ben ventured into the room to let Abby know he had the individual tea sacks ready for the ladies when they left, but since that didn't really need an announcement,

Abby suspected he just wanted to wink at Delia.

"I never did like John," Delia said as Ben left. "Your brother is a much better shopkeeper."

Abby smiled. "That's because you're sweet on him."

Delia didn't bother to deny it. "Well, he is a gentleman, and charming, witty, considerate—"

"Criminy! You make him sound like a saint."

Delia giggled. "I wouldn't go that far."

Abby didn't want to ask how *far* she had already gone, but she hoped her brother and her best friend would eventually marry. She certainly could vouch for the pleasures that married life brought. "I will admit Ben seems to be enjoying his new role."

"And he's *good* at it."

She had to agree. Like a reformed sinner, her brother scrupulously kept tabs on every penny in the till.

"Unlike that scoundrel John," Delia added with emphasis. "He wasn't quite as clever as he thought he was."

"No argument there." His fastidiousness had been his undoing. Although he had adopted a façade of merely being a shopkeeper, he hadn't been able to keep his illegal activities entirely to himself. When the authorities had gone to the rooms he rented, they'd uncovered several ledgers where he had painstakingly entered every penny from his opium trading as well as details of each laundering scheme he'd done. Luckily for his victims, he'd been somewhat of a miser. The money in his bank account—which had been confiscated—was more than enough to pay back Luke's grandmother and her friends. And Pinkerton's was now tracking down the other folks who had been swindled as well. "I'd say justice has been served."

Delia nodded. "Everything ended well."

The little bell over the front door tinkled and Abby looked up to see that Luke had entered. He stopped by the counter to talk to Ben. Whatever words were exchanged, the two of them laughed together…a far cry from when they were ready to call each other out.

Abby smiled as she watched. It was a good thing they were friends now, because in just a few months, Ben would become an uncle. And tonight, after she and Luke made love in their new home on Steiner Street, she'd tell him that he was going to be a father.

Things hadn't ended at all… The future was just beginning.

A word about the author...

Cynthia Breeding lives on the Gulf Coast of Texas with a very non-spoiled poodle-mix and enjoys walking and horseback riding on the beach, as well as sailing.

www.cynthiabreeding.com

Thank you for purchasing
this publication of The Wild Rose Press, Inc.

For questions or more information
contact us at
info@thewildrosepress.com.

The Wild Rose Press, Inc.